Stories for Peace

Stories for Peace

Seagull Books

CALCUTTA 2009

Illustrations by Anirban Ghosh, St Xavier's College, Calcutta
Cover design: Souvik Sarkar, using a detail from an illustration by Anirban Ghosh

ISBN 978 81 7046 343 6

Published by Naveen Kishore on behalf of Seagull Books Private Limited
26 Circus Avenue, Calcutta 700 017, India

Printed in India by Rockwel Offset
55B Mirza Ghalib Street, Calcutta 700 016

CONTENTS

THE BEGINNING OF THE END

Bijoyini Ganguly
18 YEARS
MAHADEVI BIRLA GIRLS' HIGHER SECONDARY SCHOOL, CALCUTTA

Once upon a time, there were two countries. Both had high mountains, scorching deserts, mysterious emerald green forests, golden fields, majestic cities, sleepy towns and picturesque hamlets.

One day, each declared war upon the other. The armies were sent out. In all directions. The two leaders had quarrelled. There was to be no compromise. The enemy must be subdued. Strategies to kill efficiently and loot smartly were planned in hushed whispers over round tables under cold lights in secret chambers of important buildings.

Preparations began in both camps. The streets, the markets, the schools and the offices rang out with one cry, 'Hail the Nation, Death to the Enemy!'

The enemy must be struck where they are most vulnerable. In one country, a brilliant colonel suggested 'the Hannibal concept': 'Let us cross the hills and attack their only unguarded mountain province.' The idea was accepted and widely appreciated. The Colonel was promoted to Major-General. A huge army was dispatched in that direction. The enemy was going to be soundly punished. They must not be allowed to raise their heads again. The mountains were going to be the first victims in this patriotic crusade of destruction. They planned to attack at daybreak.

The river gushed over the flat stones and a jackdaw perched on a low cedar branch and complained about nobody in particular. Meera dipped her feet in the running waters and tried to sing. The lone jackdaw flew away, alarmed by a human presence. Meera sang on. Her simple hill melody blended softly with the sound of the rushing river. The setting sun lit up the snowy mountains on the other side of the river and the temple bells rang out three times. The echoes lingered in the air.

Meera stopped her song and walked away.

There was a stone cottage beside the river. Inside, her mother stroked the forehead of her sleeping brother. He was only three. Meera was 14. She had work to do. She gave the two cows in the shed behind the cottage their evening meal—a mixture of husk and hay. As Meera came out, she could hear their bells softly chiming as they chewed their supper.

Her father was back from the fields on a nearby slope. It was a busy period. The planting had to be done. The seedlings must be ready when the monsoons arrived.

Meera sat down beside her father. Her mother served their evening meal from brass utensils. She put out the wood fire after they ate their rice and daal and cabbage curry. The cabbages were Meera's pride. She grew them on a small patch outside their house.

Meera got into the cot beside her brother. Her parents spread a mat on the stone floor. They piled a few sheepskin blankets, bought from a merchant from Tibet, and fell asleep. Meera lay on the cot and looked at the winking stars outside. She tried to count them. Four behind the pine tree, five beside the moon, seven in the great bear . . . her eyes grew heavy. The hut was silent except for the father's snores and a cicada that piped shrilly from the fir tree behind the cottage.

Down in the plains of Meera's country, where all the action had begun, the colours of war blazed brightly. The best brains were involved in a top-secret discussion. The attack was being discussed. In a superior twist of plans, they had decided to launch the attack in an extraordinary place. A place so far removed from the border that no one would post an army there. But it was in the heartland of enemy country. The industrial and commercial hub. An excited officer pointed at the map decorated with flags and pins. 'We have wings. We'll drop everything we've developed in our laboratories.' Heads nodded in silent agreement and the officer beamed. They would attack at night. The sleeping city would be taken unawares and the perfect 'blitzkrieg' would be launched.

The metropolis was waking up from the drowsy numbness of a hot summer day. The lights decorating the grand avenues and the expensive shops came on one by one. Long-nosed vehicles with plush upholstered seats deposited their exquisite passengers at 'The Grand'. The pride of the country. The second-largest hotel on the continent.

The banquet hall was full. Well-dressed men and women stood around with raised glasses and toasted the health of the evening's guest—Armaan K. He finished his speech and smiled at the room and wondered whether any of them understood the magnitude of his achievements. The average human mind was incapable of thinking in terms of bits and gigabytes. Armaan was an ace computer programmer and had conceptualized a computer language that could modify database storage systems forever.

Armaan left the party early. He had work to do. He drove his car through the wide roads teeming with people. He parked in front of the fourth-highest high-rise on the planet and rode the elevator to his flat on the twenty-third floor. His wife had left him, insisting he was married to his work. She was right. Armaan sat at his supercomputer and started repairing a minor bug that had emerged in his latest code.

The clock read midnight. The city was gradually retiring. Tired bodies hit the bed. The lights in Armaan's building went off, one by one. Armaan was oblivious to the world. His fingers moved swiftly over the keyboard and the lines of fantastic logic materialized on the blank screen. Armaan knew he was writing history.

What Armaan did not know was that the attack was to occur exactly 20 minutes later. The super-fast bomber jets were already circling the sleeping city. The lights glowing on the boulevards were perfect targets for their lethal cargo. The cyber-genius kept typing into the night, trying to change the world. The masked commandos were ready with the deadly missiles. The fatal countdown had begun.

Dawn was breaking over the hills. The river hurried down the slopes. The cows in the byre showed signs of awakening. Their tinkling bells could be heard. The birds heralded the sun.

Meera was back at the river-bank. She had her brother with her. She hummed another melody as he ran about on the dewy grass.

Inside the cottage, Meera's mother had set the kettle to a boil. Her father would leave for the fields after a glass of piping hot tea. Then Meera and her mother would milk the cows. After that, they would be set free. For the day. To graze on the green pastures on the slopes. At sundown, they would return to their warm byre.

Meera laughed as her brother chased a scampering squirrel. She started another song. And watched the sunbeams dance on the clear waves of the brook. Meera's brother threw pebbles into the water and was convulsed with mirth when they sunk after executing perfect ripples.

The army marched towards the valley. Meera's village was to be the first in the line of fire. Meera's world was about to end in 15 minutes. For the last time, before destruction took over, Meera's song mingled with the running river . . .

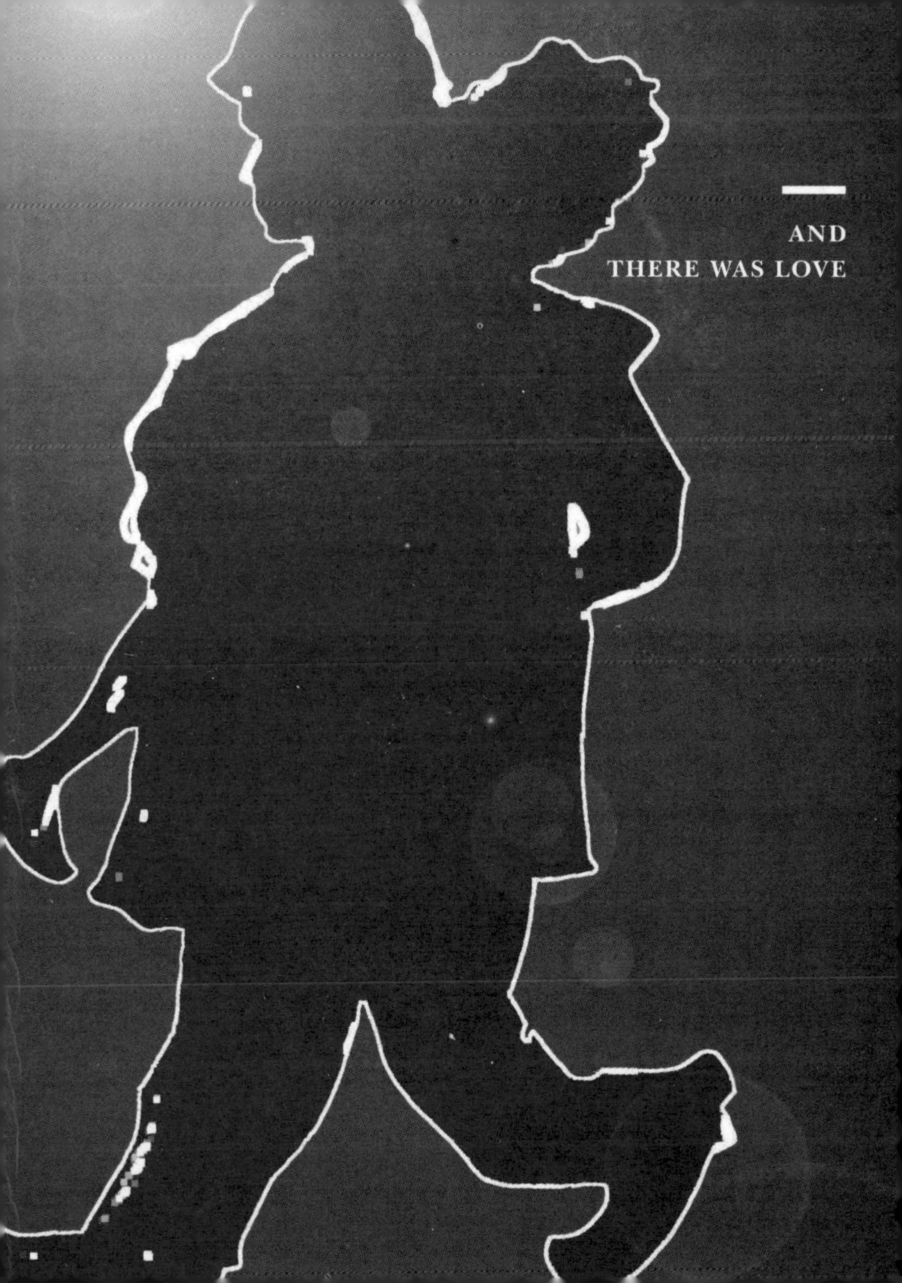

AND THERE WAS LOVE

Naomi Barton
15 YEARS
FR AGNEL MULTIPURPOSE SCHOOL, NAVI MUMBAI

She looked at him warily. She was not sure what he was, who he was, to whom he belonged or what his intentions were. She was hard, bitter, cynical and inclined to be suspicious at the slightest thing. She was four years old. She stood up as straight as a maypole, as solemn as a priest, her hair blowing in the wind stained by Hitler's breath, and the helpless, desperate screams of those who knew not where to run, where to hide, when death had already bound their terrified hearts with its rope of German hands.

She fixed her older-than-four-years-old knowing eyes on him. She had forgotten how to hope, even though the 'war' was over, even though she ought not to have. He looked at her curiously. Wondered idly in his mind why they were trying to eradicate the Jews if all little Jewish girls were like this one, when this one was like every innocent little girl ever born. He knelt down, to look into her eyes, and in halting, broken English, asked her, 'Where are your mamma–pappa, little one?' She looked at him objectively and asked, in turn, 'Will you tell me, please? They went with the big noise, and I'm looking for them.' He looked at the poor thing pityingly. Nowhere to go, no one to go to, forever to hold nothing, to die unmourned. He, a straying German soldier, tried to smile at her.

He failed. He told her he was sorry, because her mamma and pappa had gone to a happier, nicer place. They thought she would like it here, and they would come back another time to pick her up and take her with them, to the happy, nice place. She stared at him and said, 'Liar.' She turned and looked around her, at the carnage, at the wreck of what once was her haven, her home, her happy place. 'They wouldn't leave me behind in this. They're not gone either. They're just . . .' And an awful, burning, choking silence filled the air. He didn't have to give a damn about that little morsel of what would have been, but he did. And ached for her Lost World.

He picked her up. She didn't struggle. She had no reason to live, and none to die. She just . . . was. Another remnant. Another 'POW'. Another wreck. War was over, remember? It was time to rejoice! To hope again! Yes . . .

So he picked her up. And walked. And walked. A little light came into her sorrowful eyes. She remembered her pappa holding her like this. Smiling, throwing her up in the air, while she shrieked with laughter, a little diamond spilling out of a bluey-white sky. She felt a little better. And the soldier thought about what he was to do. A poor German soldier carrying a little Jewish girl, to a home maybe, a somewhere for her to go, to take the huge, colossal, humbling responsibility of being her someone to go to. And lifted her a little higher.

I'm the old, wrinkled man standing there and watching, you see. The old, old man, who was to die even before death came knocking. So it didn't matter. And I wondered what that twisted, sick person, who began this fruitless futile war, would think of this little scene, this magnificently perverse, yet beautiful bit of Anti-Jewism. Ha! It was heartening, you know. And saddening at the same time. That it took a war such as this one to bring about this truth. Amazing, isn't it, humanity?! Some kill, slaughter and laugh, and some quietly hold the same thing another would kill, to begin again, to give life again. I laugh at the complex simplicity of it. And try not to cry . . .

BROKEN DREAMS

Urmika Agarwal
14 YEARS
BIRLA HIGH SCHOOL (GIRLS' SECTION), CALCUTTA

1949. The boy was sitting outside, near a small hill. 'So much peace and calm everywhere,' he thought to himself as he looked on at the green trees. Their leaves, blowing softly in the wind. 'Everywhere but here!' he screamed.

He was crying. Frustrated and confused, he tried to forget it all but the pictures kept flashing across his mind. He was lost—lost in the crowd. He was crying aloud for his parents and his sister, but they were nowhere. His pleas for help were drowned by the yelling of the crowd. Why were people killing each other? There was blood everywhere. His left arm hurt. 'Mother!' he screamed. Houses were on fire. Dead bodies lay everywhere. 'Mother!' he screamed, again and again and the world spun, round and round . . .

A gentleman rescued him, tried to console him but he was determined not to listen. His arm was wrapped in a dirty cloth to stop the blood. 'My parents aren't dead,' he told the man angrily. 'They're out there, looking for me. Thank you for your help, but I must go now,' he said, agitated.

'You're not going anywhere,' said the man. 'Accept it—your parents are no more.' The boy ran out, refused to eat, refused to accept the fact that he was left with no one and nothing but his thoughts.

As night came, he wondered why people fought. He asked the man. The man said they fought because of the differences in their religions. 'But what is the difference? We are all God's children, aren't we? Then why? Why does everyone have so much hatred in their hearts?' the boy asked, frustrated.

'Son, only you feel this way. You surprise me. You are so young, yet you know so much about life. I will protect you for as long as you want me to, I promise you that.'

'You're a Pakistani, I'm a Hindu. Yet you accept me?' the boy asked, irritated by the man's calm words.

'I don't believe in religion. I believe in one race—the human race—created by God. You can only conquer the world with patience and peace, son,' the man replied.

'Like it?' the boy asked. 'Yes, it's good,' the man answered, smiling. He slowly sipped his tea and thought about the past. Fifteen years had gone by. The boy and the man had opened up a little shop together in a small district in India. Forced to move to India because of the riots, they had grown very close to each other over the years. Now they were back in Pakistan, after all this time.

The boy walked around, reminiscing, trying to think happy thoughts. But the livid memories, smouldering, red, suddenly flashed across his eyes. He sat down. Slowly the tears came. He wept. Not out of sorrow, but because he had finally found tranquility. He had found peace. God had not forgotten about him. He believed he was God's child—God had come to him as the old man.

He had learnt so much from the old man. Above all, he had learnt the true meaning of peace. 'It is everywhere—no matter what the circumstance. You just have to look a little closer, a little deeper into yourself.'

BROKEN MUSIC

Aparna Chaudhuri
18 YEARS
CALCUTTA GIRLS' HIGH SCHOOL, CALCUTTA

It was early evening.

The air of Paranthewali Gali, usually heavy with grease, was crisp and fresh after an unexpected afternoon shower and beginning to fill with the aroma of kebabs. Children, released from the confinement of the rain-hours, ran shrieking through the street, boisterous again.

The Ustaad would have liked to linger as he normally did—enticed, not by the kebabs, but by the general succulence of the scene, the sizzling of meat and oil and spices, the blaze of naked bulbs and kerosene lanterns against the soft twilight, the children, the flecks of kites in the rain-washed sky, the soft film of shadow beginning to steal over and soften the harsh colours and jutting angles of one of the city's poorer quarters. Indeed, his steps had involuntarily slowed and his fingers begun to draw a noiseless Puriya from the light bamboo sarangi concealed under his shawl. But today he curbed that desire and continued his slow, ambling, but not directionless, progress towards Chandni Chowk, managing to reach the busy heart of Delhi in not much more than 10 unnecessary minutes.

Here, however, the old sarangi-player stood transfixed, watching the ebb and flow of the evening crowd, the animated give-and-take of commerce, the moth-like movement of women through the brilliant maze. Soon, his free hand stole to his pocket. There it encountered a dirty scrap of paper onto which he began diffidently, in his unpractised writing, to transfer the choked, halting poetry of a *bandish* forming in his head.

When he finally reached the lion-headed pillars and wrought-iron gate of Vasant Vilas, it was almost seven. Krishnaraj Pandit, the cultured head of the old and eminent Pandit family, was waiting, his face betraying a mixture of alarm and resignation. Seeing his revered guest shuffle uncertainly up the shallow, curving steps, however, he stepped forward quickly, hands outstretched, head bowed, in a gesture of unfeigned respect.

'*Aiye*, *aiye*, Ustaad Sahib—we thought you had lost your way! I was on the point of sending the car—' He gracefully conducted the Ustaad through the rooms to the wide portico at the back. The fragrance of jasmine and *raat-ki-rani*, newly awakened by the rain, never failed to delight the old man. He closed his eyes, his lined, yet childlike face a picture of delight. 'Truly, Pandit Sahib, you have created paradise for me to play in!'

'Our guests,' said Krishnaraj Pandit. 'They have been waiting to hear your music.'

The Ustaad opened his eyes and smiled at his feet. Then he made his usual hesitant *adaab*. 'They do me great honour.'

This brief exchange appeared to exhaust him, and he sank onto the thick Kashmiri carpet laid out for the recital. As he meticulously tuned his sarangi, his listeners arranged themselves in a rapt half-circle around the bent, gnome-like form.

The tuning complete, he played a few runs up and down the scale—a quick *palta*—then appeared to fall into a reverie, stroking the strings of the sarangi with a finger, and pulling thoughtfully on one ear. After about 10 minutes of uncertainty, Krishnaraj Pandit couldn't bear it any longer. To interrupt the thoughts of such a great musician was undoubtedly a liberty. Then again, the Ustaad could be relied upon to not take offence, nor even to regard it as anything but a perfectly reasonable question even if (to him) obtrusive and irrelevant.

'Pardon me, Ustaad Sahib, but which raag will we be privileged to hear today?'

His question fell on deaf ears. The Ustaad was gazing with interest and affection at a small boy in the audience, the five-year-old son of one of Krishnaraj's brothers.

'Did you see the kites being flown today?' he asked the boy.

The youngster, obviously under strict instructions to keep quiet, squirmed uncomfortably.

The Ustaad went on. 'There was a red one with a blue stripe and a yellow one with a green spot. The two were chasing each other. The yellow kite seemed to be outwitting the red—but then there was a sudden gust, and the red one jerked on its string. Next thing I saw, the yellow one was fluttering to the ground.' The boy nodded gravely.

'What's your name, son?' asked the Ustaad.

After a few moments of intense fidgeting, the child whispered conspiratorially, 'Pilu.'

The Ustaad was delighted. 'Pilu,' he repeated with the air of one making the most private of confidences. Then, this time to the assembly, 'Pilu.'

The audience looked aghast. Krishnaraj Pandit tried manfully to meet the eye of a connoisseur of music whose every feature registered frank horror at the thought of Raag Pilu being played at seven in the evening. Mercifully, the Ustaad's actions belied his words—the notes of an impeccable Marwa were already beginning to issue from his instrument, drawn forth by loving fingers and released to mingle with the firefly-lit evening air.

After the recital, Krishnaraj Pandit had the family Buick brought round to take the Ustaad home.

The Ustaad gazed at the car, unseeing. Then, before anyone could stop him, he walked around it and out into the warm night. For once, his host attempted to follow him.

'It isn't safe for you, Ustaad Sahib. The roads around Suiwalan—at this time of night—' He looked at the Ustaad's long black *angarakha*, the cap on the untidy thatch of grey hair. He did not, of course, expect the Ustaad to be remotely conscious of the prevailing tension between the Hindu and Muslim localities of the city. But he had not foreseen the Ustaad's firm resistance to his request.

'*Kabhi nahin*, Pandit Sahib, I will walk home. It's such a peaceful night.'

'Ustaad Sahib, forgive me, but your safety—'

'Can't play Kedara in a car.' The Ustaad smiled puckishly and adjusted the bamboo sarangi under his shawl.

The next morning, after *riyaaz*, the Ustaad was sipping tea on a charpoy in the courtyard, when his nephew emerged from the rooms of the *mardana* and stood in front of him.

The Ustaad gazed at the young man with affection—dearer to him, this Rahim, than any of his own sons, though he would never have admitted the fact. Tall, fair, long-limbed, he towered over his frail uncle and his strong features held nothing of the puckered abstraction of the Ustaad's, yet the ears—the ears stuck out just a little, prompting others to note a resemblance . . .

Rahim's devotion to music heartened his uncle, his gentle, affectionate manner endeared him to his aunts, the younger children adored him, but it was with his cousin, the Ustaad's eldest son, that Rahim shared the strongest bond. Both 21, both raised from early childhood within the enchanted circle of music that was the centre of this otherwise noisy and crowded household, they were the Ustaad's two dearest disciples. Yet physically so dissimilar: Rahim tall and fair, Karim slight and dark. Unlike in manner, too: Rahim affectionate, easygoing, Karim brooding and withdrawn. 'Pancham and Rishabh,' the Ustaad had concluded. One open, strong; the other full of a subdued mystery. One reassuring in its constancy; the other shifting, unpredictable. One like the rising sun, the other twilight.

But when they were together, the contrasts seemed to merge, become a harmonious whole—like Raag Desh, as the

Ustaad often thought—like two melodic counterpoints, balancing and complementing each other. Technically, Karim was the better player but Rahim played with more *dil*. Despite his imperfections, he would never be a *baseet*.

Of course, in his heart of hearts, the Ustaad knew why he held Rahim so dear—and there was an element of anxiety in that otherwise perfect love. He remembered his Mamu—a hard taskmaster and a hard man. He remembered the hours of practice, the relentless criticism, the constant curbing of his ardour. He remembered them without rancour. Mamu had given him his earliest and deepest musical insights, but some long-suppressed remnant of rebelliousness made him yearn for memories of a freer adolescence and inwardly resolve never to discipline his own nephew so sternly.

Karim now appeared—suddenly, as always—and stood beside Rahim. The Ustaad struggled to remember what he had meant to tell them.

'Last night I was—' he stopped and tried to collect his thoughts from straying around a meditative Puriya Kalyan.

'Yes, Abba-jaan?' Prompted Karim.

'I was coming home from the *baithak* at—'

'Pandit Sahib's, Mama-jaan,' supplied Rahim.

'Yes, yes, and I saw two young men following me down the road—right after I turned the corner at that *halwai's*— whatshis-name—and I thought it might be you two. I meant to call out, but I was practising that fast *taan*—' He hummed a few notes, hoarsely.

'But it wasn't us, Abba-jaan,' said Karim, puzzled.

'Hmmm—what was I saying? Yes, so what I want to know is, why didn't you come home with me instead of following me like a pair of shadows? In any case, I thought you'd be at evening *riyaaz*?' The Ustaad, having delivered the burden of his intended homily, sank gratefully back into Puriya Kalyan.

'Mama-jaan,' said Rahim clearly. 'It wasn't us. We were at home all evening.'

'Not you? Then who could it have been?' For the first time since seeing those shadowy forms emerge from a maze of by-lanes and trail him silently home, the Ustaad experienced a faint feeling of fear.

The cousins exchanged nervous glances. It would be useless to try and convince the Ustaad that, in this year of riots and massacres, 1947, strolling home at midnight through areas fraught with communal tension was hardly wise. Suiwalan itself was primarily a Hindu area. Generally beloved though the

Ustaad was, every member of his family feared for his life when he walked alone through its streets at night.

'It was that damned Bal,' said Karim privately to his cousin that night. 'I heard him boast he'd knife every Mussalman in Delhi if he had the chance.'

Rahim's face was in shadow, but his long, lounging form stiffened visibly.

'Of course, Bal's vicious and a coward. But you can't blame him for saying what he did, when you consider that five *galis* away some Mussalman is threatening to do the same to every Hindu he can find.'

'What's that got to do with us?' asked Rahim abruptly.

Karim frowned at the change in his cousin's tone. 'Rahim, you idiot, do you mean to start a riot?'

Rahim shrugged.

'Once the killing starts, it'll never stop, can't you see? And we'll come off worst in the end—we'll lose everything we have, you fool. What's wrong with the way we've lived all these years? What have we against them, or they against us?'

'So why was Mama-jaan followed?' asked Rahim sarcastically. 'Those youths wanted to pay their respects to him, I suppose?'

'You're a totally different person these days, Rahim' said Karim, deliberately. 'Just because Abba doesn't see the change in you, don't think I can't.'

'What's the use, when you're blind to everything else?'

Rahim stormed out of the room in a rage. A little later, Karim heard the scrape of the outer door being unbarred.

Riots broke out that night—and Rahim did not return.

Karim and his uncle, the Ustaad's younger brother, locked and barred every door. Lights were blown out—in the darkness, the women left the *zenana* and crowded into the innermost storeroom. They were locked in, and Karim's uncle stood guard by the door. Through a single crack in a street facing window, the Ustaad's old servant, Aslam, tremblingly watched the tumult outside.

Karim, entering his father's room, tried to keep the fear out of his voice.

'No, Abba-jaan, he hasn't come back, but he will soon. He must be at some friend's house. He's quite right not to venture out while the trouble lasts. He'll be back in the morning.'

Through the darkness, he could see his father trembling. Screams filtered through the walls—Karim made the mistake of closing his eyes and instantly felt himself at the heart of the riot.

Beside him, the Ustaad shook even more violently, his breath coming in gasps, 'Rahim—Rahim—'

'Quiet, Abba!' whispered Karim urgently.

The mob was approaching their door. Steady screaming from the street welled up in Karim's ears—the smell of blood rose through the clammy floor. Any moment now, the hail of blows on the door would be cut short by the splintering crash of an axe, they would be dragged out of their hiding places and separately butchered, or the house would simply be set on fire . . .

Caught in the eye of the storm, the house waited.

At dawn, everyone fell into an exhausted sleep. Only Karim stayed awake, waiting for Rahim to return. The enforced patience that had lasted him all night deserted him within minutes now.

He unbolted a back door, slipped out, wedged the door shut as firmly as possible, and looked up and down the street.

A street of the dead, with the uneasy peace of a morgue hanging over it.

Rahim—no, it couldn't be. He was so unnerved he was imagining things. Any moment now, and he would see Rahim hurrying up the street towards him, anxious to know how they had survived the night.

Rahim, my brother, it is impossible that you who were so angry and alive last evening should be this blood-stained, fire-blackened corpse at my feet now.

Or if it is you, you are not dead, merely very badly injured and frightened. The burn cannot be so bad if I can see your face through it—the face my father preferred to my own. All that blood on your kurta cannot possibly be from the gash in your chest.

Rahim, if you are dead, I have killed you, because I was the one who sent you out into the riot last night.

'Rahim!' Karim could not stifle the cry that seared his throat. The riot engulfed him and he ran, through bloody streets under a threatening sky, avoiding the piled corpses, the charred rubble, ran from the dead Rahim, ran in the hope of finding a place where Rahim would be alive again, his face unscarred, his body whole, more perfect than his own could ever be, igniting the familiar, momentary blaze of jealousy . . .

Spring. The harsingar in the garden was blooming, the ground underneath frosted with blossoms. Raag Basant spilled like rich water from the Ustaad's sarangi. As long as he kept playing, he was safe, drowned in a deep well of peace . . .

Less than five kilometers away, the first trainload of refugees rumbled out of Old Delhi Station and turned its face towards Karachi.

Basant to Bahar. Bahar to Hindol. The music was loosening its hold . . .

Opening his eyes, the Ustaad blinked as he found himself looking into the troubled face of Krishnaraj Pandit. It did not occur to him to question his presence.

'*Adaab*, Pandit Sahib.'

'You were playing, Ustaad Sahib. It seems as if I have not heard your sarangi for a year. May I listen a little longer?'

'It is not easy these days, Pandit Sahib,' the Ustaad's voice faltered, 'There's a tremor in my hands—and I remember things—'

'We all do.'

For a while, there was silence, as the two men sat in the empty courtyard amid the echoing rooms.

'I have come to beg a favour, Ustaad Sahib,' said Krishnaraj Pandit at last.

'Is there anything I can grant anyone anymore?'

'It is that you will honour me by residing in my house till this trouble blows over and your family returns from Pakistan.'

'Forgive me, Pandit Sahib.'

'Ustaad Sahib, there are worse times ahead. In Bengal, they attempted to assassinate the Viceroy yesterday. There are riots in Punjab. Four thousand people have been killed in Lucknow. Delhi's the worst—there could be a riot beginning on the street outside this very minute. For the sake of your family, Ustaad Sahib, for the sake of your music, come with me.'

'I cannot risk your family's lives for the sake of my own, Pandit Sahib,' mumbled the Ustaad.

'They will come to no harm. No one will know. No one will suspect you're there. I will make every arrangement—'

'Forgive me, Pandit Sahib, but it is impossible.'

'Ustaad Sahib, you don't understand.'

'I understand that this is my destiny.'

'No—'

'Yes.'

The finality of his tone startled Krishnaraj Pandit.

'How can I explain, Pandit Sahib? You will not understand, for all your kindness—' The old hesitancy returned to the Ustaad's tone. 'I am not a very good Muslim. I forget the times for *namaaz*. When I am practising, I hear only the sound of the sarangi, not the call of *azaan*. I have done this for years. Now, within a single week, I bury one son and lose the other. All I can think is that Allah is punishing me.'

'No Ustaad Sahib, that cannot be—'

'I used to think so too, Pandit Sahib. All these years, whenever I felt frightened by the thought of my sins, I comforted myself by thinking of music. I told myself the music was pure, and Allah could not blame me for seeking it. I told myself I had found peace in music because Allah willed it. It was wrong of me, Pandit Sahib—I know that now—but it was so perfect, that peace, and it lasted more than 50 years—how could I tell, Pandit Sahib, how could I ever tell how wrong it was?'

'Forgive me, Ustaad Sahib, but you are wrong now—your music is the gift of Allah.'

'But I never repaid the debt, Pandit Sahib!'

A leaf, brown, and curling at the edges, floated past on an eddy of air. The Ustaad put out his hand to catch it, but something failed in him—his hand remained outstretched, palm upward, in a gesture of entreaty.

'Every falling leaf was part of that peace, Pandit Sahib. Every bird. Every lane around this house. Every dawn and twilight.'

His voice seemed to be coming from very far away.

'Every swirl of dust in summer, every slant of rain.'

'Every child—in your house, in my own. My daughters. Rahim. Karim.'

'They were all fragments of my peace, Pandit Sahib—each fragment a whole.'

'They are not lost, Ustaad Sahib,' said Krishnaraj Pandit gently. 'They will come back to you.'

'You are right, Pandit Sahib. They will come back—some day —when the country is divided and the old people gone and the young ones changed. When no one has any time to make music or to listen to it. And there are some who will never return, Pandit Sahib—some who have gone forever, and my peace has gone with them.'

'No, Ustaad Sahib—you will forget—'

'But that is merely oblivion, Pandit Sahib. Opium brings an old man oblivion—but can it bring him peace? I too am old, Pandit Sahib, too old to gather stones together, too old to build my peace again, but I would rather not take opium and lose even the memory of peace.'

A few more leaves fell. The dust of the unswept courtyard stirred and sighed.

Krishnaraj Pandit hesitated, then bowed his head. 'Then, Ustaad Sahib, permit me to arrange for you to join your relatives in Karachi. Despite everything you have said, I cannot remember your music and leave you here.'

The Ustaad did not reply, and Krishnaraj Pandit knew his words had not reached the old man's ears. He pressed his hands briefly, and stood up to leave. Without the sarangi on his shoulder, the bent figure on the cot seemed even smaller than before.

All day and all night, the Ustaad remained on his charpoy in the courtyard. The dust of the troubled street fell on his clothes, his hair, gathered undisturbed on his sarangi.

In his study at Vasant Vilas, Krishnaraj Pandit picked up the telephone receiver, intending to make a trunk call to Karachi. A faint crackling came down the line, like the tension of summer air waiting for a storm.

Like the dust stirring around the bowed figure in the silent courtyard.

Like the last breath of withered leaves clinging to a tree.

He replaced the receiver on its cradle, sat down and sighed.

CLOUDS

Devaki Ghose
16 YEARS
SOUTH POINT HIGH SCHOOL, CALCUTTA

Shalini sat by her windowsill and gazed out into the twilight. The last blush of pink was fading on the distant horizon and a strange, sullen darkness was waiting to take over. Clouds, dark and heavy, flocked in from the eastern corner. Then the wind rose, a wind that shook the trees with a monstrous force and that roared like an angry beast. 'So here's rain at last,' thought Shalini. She was tired of this damn place and the damn heat. The summer months had stretched endlessly—a stifling, dry spell. But as the mercury soared higher and higher and the heat became more and more unbearable, she had a strong and jubilant expectation—a few more days and there'd be the rain. 'And I was right,' she mused to herself as she looked outside.

Somehow the darkness of the place, the cloudy ambience, reminded her of a day 18 years ago and she fell into nostalgic reverie.

She had been only seven then, and it had been a dreary and cold January morning. Just like today, the clouds had hung low over everything—the green meadows, the tops of the sky-high Hindu Kush, the crystal-clear, blue waters of the Karumbar lake. They had known a snowstorm was approaching, yet, with childish zeal, she and Naaz had gone out into the open. She would never forget that day. The catastrophic blizzard, the monstrous winds brutally pulling at them, the numbing cold and the heavy snowfall—all seared into her memory. Never again would she dare to venture out in a blizzard! How she and Naaz were scolded!

Ah Naaz . . . her childhood companion, her inseparable playmate, now a precious jewel of her lost childhood! They had spent many a happy day, running and chasing each other in the meadows by the ever-so-blue waters of the Karumbar. Watched the magic of the sunrise atop the majestic Hindu Kush . . . the soft glow, the golden ethereal light dancing on the tops of the slender chinars, then waking the sleeping flowers in the meadows and, at last, igniting the saffron fields in a blaze of burning gold! And there were others too—Boonyi, Raazan, Ali, her classmates in the local school . . . They'd walk through the intoxicating, blinding red of the poppy fields, past Pandit Bhatt's apple orchards to that little wooden school. She didn't remember the lessons but the memories of the festivities, of Shivratri, Dusshera and Bakr-Id, were still vivid in her memory. How she missed the smells of the delectable Wazwaan meal and the accompanying *bhand pather* (clown stories) and plays enacted during the festivities.

'It is a divine privilege that we are born Kashmiri. You feast and you celebrate during Shivratri and Id alike. Our cultures and religions intermingle, mutate, evolve and enrich themselves through co-existence,' her father used to say. Co-existence indeed! How downright hypocritical! What she knew and hated to acknowledge in public was the fact that she was a Kashmiri Pandit, a fact that invariably provoked responses such as 'Oh, I'm so sorry' or 'Oh you have such a glorious past!' For god's sake, pity was the last thing she wanted! Why was she displaced from her idyllic village 17 years ago? Wasn't it because she belonged to a Kashmiri Pandit family and didn't go to a mosque?

1990. Mullahs with long beards preached in mosques—'Kashmiri Pandits, leave this place for good!' It was happening again . . . her indelible past was taking over her emotions once again, again the memories came floating in . . . hundreds of

Kashmiri homes burnt . . . lakhs of Pandits fleeing . . . the refugee camps . . . and, at last, this small housing on the outskirts of Delhi, this sprawling metropolis far away from her paradise and her homeland! Oh Naaz! They had gone to their home to say goodbye but they were so frightened to talk to them that they wouldn't even open the doors. After all this, I'd never go back there, never, thought Shalini. In Delhi, though I lie torn between two identities I still have a life. I study at the university and my friends love me. Collecting her thoughts and pulling herself together, she emerged from her reverie.

Then she saw it. The clouds were no longer there—they were drifting away northwards. So it was just a trick that they had played on her. It would be that heat again!

Shalini rose gloomily from her seat and cooked a simple dinner of dal and chapattis for herself and her ailing parents. She was silent during dinner and went to bed early.

The next morning she woke up to the news that a strong wind had pushed the clouds northward. It had snowed heavily in the Hindu Kush and the northern part of Pakistan Occupied Kashmir. According to the MET Office, the monsoon had been delayed in northern India by a couple of weeks. 'Aha couple of weeks, pretty short time, *na*?' she thought sarcastically. 'Clouds, those incorrigible, wayward wanderers—how dare they go where they please? If we can divide territories and raise boundaries on land, why not cut up the sky? Why not dam the rivers and oceans? The clouds are sponging up water from *our* lakes and rivers to shower over *their* land while we rot in the searing heat!' . . . Once again, her mind wandered off to her homeland. Perhaps it was snowing there. Perhaps the white snowflakes were falling on the flaming red of the poppy fields, the burning gold of the saffron, the tops of the majestic pines and chinars. The tall trees, like sacred hermits in their new cloaks of white, were reaching out for the heavens yet clinging to the soil of their birth. The whole place was blanketed in snow, perhaps basking in the sunlight . . . oh, the light was too bright to look at!

Lost in her thoughts, she looked out of the window. It must be noon. The sun was climbing up the sky, over the skyscrapers. The snow must be melting out there, flake by flake. The sky, clearing up. Perhaps the sun was shining brightly over the crystal clear landscape of her homeland, snow-washed and pure. Her white pony, dear little Yasmin, whom she had abandoned in the meadows, was munching fresh grass by the Karumbar. Perhaps she was no more, but her calves were there—new life, hopeful and innocent of the dark past. 'Oh how could I, even in my thoughts, betray my childhood?' thought Shalini. No, Nature is infinitely wiser than us. Let the clouds roam free. Perhaps a day will come when she too will be free to go back to the place of her dreams—green as ever.

COMING HOME

Nayantara Nayar
15 YEARS
LADY ANDAL SCHOOL, CHENNAI

29 SEPTEMBER, 2 A.M.

'Get down doctor!' cried a man. She threw herself to the ground as a car behind her exploded.

She stifled a scream. What was wrong with them?! This was a neutral area!

She crawled across the mud to one of the soldiers and demanded angrily, 'What's going on?! Since when do they attack a hospital zone?'

'I don't know, Ma'am. I think the Peace Conference didn't go very well.'

She frowned, 'Again? What are they doing? Don't they realize that every time they squabble their own men are dying?' He looked blankly at her and she sighed, 'Well, I want you to tell the General that I have enough patients.' Then she stood up and strode into the makeshift hospital tents, her mouth a thin line, her eyes grim.

26 OCTOBER, 5.30 P.M.

The doctor looked up as the flap opened. Her face hardened—her newest patients wasn't a day older than 17. His arm lay limp by his side and his face was as pale as a sheet. She told the soldiers where to put him and to find him a nurse or doctor.

Why was she still getting so many patients? It had been a week since the latest cease-fire had been ordered. Usually, the number of patients decreased.

She gazed at the tent flap but her mind was elsewhere. At that very moment another conference was in progress. A group of crotchety old men, who smoked too much, were sitting in outsized chairs and bargaining over the lives of these men! Bargaining with lives that meant nothing to them. And for what? For one miserable strip of land. She knew the only way she'd ever forgive her father was if the land was left alone.

She snapped back to reality when she heard a groan. She turned to see the boy who had just come in gesturing wildly. She ran across and knelt beside him.

He coughed loudly and muttered something.

'Did he fight in the last battle, near Reisch?' she asked.

The nurse nodded and helped her stop the young soldier from thrashing about in his cot.

'All right—ready?' the nurse nodded, 'Good.' She moved the boy's left arm onto the bed. The scream that followed soon after was barely audible in the surrounding chaos.

27 OCTOBER, 1 A.M.

She wiped her brow and dropped into a chair. She looked around the tent and was happy to see that it was quiet. Well, as quiet as it could ever be. At least, there weren't any emergency cases.

She reached for a mug and gulped down as much water as she could. She longed for a little rest, but knew she couldn't until she'd finished the other two tents. She put down the mug and walked outside.

Soldiers were standing guard, there grim faces weary and drawn. She sighed and made her way to the next tent.

Inside, there was utter chaos. The tent was overflowing with the dead and dying. She ordered all the able-bodied soldiers to carry out the dead and cremate them. Then she started to work.

She looked towards the end of the tent and saw Corporal Harin sitting next to the large radio set and raised her eyebrows.

'I'm sorry, Doctor. No messages.'

She nodded sadly and turned back to her patients. In the middle of the tent was another new arrival. She'd seen him when they'd brought him in but hadn't had time to check whether he was worth saving. She needed to know how he was wounded. A bullet was all right, but if he was a gas victim he was as good as dead. Trying to save him would be pointless. Brutal but practical. War left little room for anything else.

She bent over him and was relieved to find him conscious.

'Sergeant Gavin—that's your name isn't it? I'm sorry but I need to talk to you.'

His eyes fluttered open and he coughed, 'Yes, Ma'am.'

'I need to know how your leg was injured.'

'It was a bullet, Ma'am.'

She looked at him in relief. 'Then you'll be all right. But your fever is worrying. I'll just—' She was about to call a nurse when he asked in a low voice 'Is it true? Is there a chance that we can go home?' She smiled, a little sadly and said, 'Hopefully.'

'Ma'am, do you think it will ever stop?'

She looked at him thoughtfully, 'Maybe, but all wars are the same, which is why there are so many. At the beginning it's for some cause, then for power and prestige, then it's just because they don't know how to stop.'

He nodded, his eyes sad.

She wanted to reassure him—tell him he would see his loved ones again—so she sat on her knees and took his hand, 'Don't worry, Sergeant, it will stop. Maybe we'll get to experience this thing they call peace.' He nodded again and his eyes began to droop. She left him and made her way to the radio station.

'Haven't they said anything?! Don't they at least have the decency to tell us whether or not these men are going to die?' she asked Corporal Harin, her voice angry, her eyes blazing.

A pair of calm, brown eyes met hers and she felt ashamed, realizing he didn't deserve to suffer for their mistakes.

'I'm sorry, Corporal. I know you can't do anything.'

He looked at her thoughtfully and said quietly, 'No, Ma'am, I can't, but you have a right to be angry. You're a doctor, someone who values life beyond everything else, someone like you has to make decisions like this. You should go home, Doctor. It'd ease a lot of people's minds, especially your father's.'

'When they end this stupid war, I'll go home.'

He shook his head, about to say something when she shushed him.

'Wha—?'

'Quiet! Turn it up, they're announcing something, Corporal!' she said, her voice urgent.

Silence. She looked behind her and saw that everyone, every soldier, doctor and nurse, was staring at the radio.

She was about to tell them to get back to work when a familiar voice shattered the silence.

'People of Arag. This is your President! I am happy to say that today's conference was successful!'

'It's the President . . . ' 'Successful? Does that mean . . . ' 'Oh bless President Shamith!' She signalled for silence and bent to raise the volume. '. . . and so a treaty has been reached. Both countries have agreed to support the World Peace Committee's resolution and peace has been declared. I know that this war has taken sons away from mothers, husbands from wives, and fathers from daughters. You came when your country called and we are proud. I can't say that you shall never be called upon again, but peace has always been preferable to war. We shall strive to achieve a world where there are no armies and wars. We shall strive to make our world safe without guns and happy without greed.'

'Once a little girl told me that she wanted to make the world better. I told her I would help, and now I intend to. That is our goal.' His powerful voice paused for a moment, then continued smoothly, 'I want all troops to return home as soon as possible! That is an official order! I repeat all sons, husbands, fathers and . . .' his voice hesitated, '. . . and daughters are to come home. We are waiting for you.'

She smiled at the speech and wanted to hug someone. She restrained herself and turned to see various nurses and doctors holding on to each other and crying. Soldiers were weeping like broken children. Outside, they were shouting in joy. It was over—after three years of violence, pain and death, it was over. Now, there was just peace. She smiled at her staff and couldn't help wanting to repeat the word, 'Peace . . .'

1 NOVEMBER, 4 A.M.

She walked around the tent, a nurse beside her. 'How many have survived the week?' the nurse questioned, her voice low and soft. 'Not all, but more than I expected. We were lucky,' the doctor replied.

The nurse sighed and stopped at a bed. She began to gently scold a soldier, 'You shouldn't be up, your fever may be down but you need rest if you want to go home . . .'

On a bed a few feet away, Sergeant Gavin was waiting for her to come towards him. His bullet wound was healing fast and his fever was gone. He had been about to call out when he realized he didn't know the doctor's name. When he thought about it he'd never heard anyone call her other than Ma'am, even though she seemed younger than most of the soldiers there.

She stopped near his bed and smiled. 'Are you awake? Your fever isn't back is it?'

'No Ma'am, don't worry,' he replied, 'I just wanted to see if it was true. Some soldiers were saying that patients in a stable condition were going home soon.'

She smiled, 'Yes, soldiers who are well enough are going home.'

He was about to ask whether he were one of those soldiers, but she cut him off, still smiling, 'You're on that list, Sergeant.'

He grinned, his eyes bright, 'It seems you were right, Ma'am.'

'Oh?' she asked with a raised eyebrow.

'It all did stop. They finally figured out how to stop.'

She laughed, 'Yes, I suppose they did.'

'Just a moment, Doctor. I need to know your name. Your work here has been very important to the men. I think they'd want to know to whom they owe their lives.'

She laughed and then looked embarrassed 'No need. After all, it's not only me.'

The Sergeant shook his head stubbornly, 'No, Ma'am. I know you were in charge of the entire camp's hospital site. And you were not ordered here—you volunteered. And that deserves recognition.'

She shrugged, 'I came here because I can help heal. Isn't that the first step towards peace?'

He nodded.

She gazed at him thoughtfully, 'If you're going to lose sleep over it then you may as well know. The staff call me Doctor Shamith.'

GIVE PEACE A CHANCE

Tania Kathuria
18 YEARS
BIRLA HIGH SCHOOL (GIRLS' SECTION), CALCUTTA

A bright sunny morning. 15th August, Independence Day. Little did the tiny tots know what a dreadful fate awaited them. Dressed in vibrant colours, they were playing near the beautiful lake. The sun's rays were falling on the water, and the shimmer was reflected in their bright faces. Their innocent eyes dazzled as they dreamt of the magnificent evening ahead of them, though some of them were a bit nervous about their performance. After all, they had been rehearsing for this day for months. The Chief Minister of Kashmir himself had agreed to be the Chief Guest for this grand celebration.

Far from this peaceful corner of the earth, in the depths of a dark forest, five masterminds were plotting to set the school ablaze. It was a meticulous plan. Everything was in place and nothing could stop them now. They were carrying gifts for the children and bouquets for the teachers and Chief Guest. The beauty of the gifts conveniently hid their cruel contents. The men marched towards their destination, determined.

Though high-security measures had been put in place, the men, posing as school staff and carrying fake identity cards, easily slipped past them. Once they'd crossed the cordons, they assembled the bombs they had smuggled in and set them in every nook and corner of the building.

Soon, it was time for the much-awaited programme to start. The Chief Minister had arrived. The children recited poems, danced to patriotic tunes and put up a play on how to bring about peace between the two nations.

The leader of the gang was watching the performance. Slowly, he grew engrossed in it. But then he realized it was nothing more than a mere play—far from the truth of life. He walked out of the auditorium. Far away, he saw a little girl, sitting all by herself, trying to paint.

'What are you trying to do?'

Uncle, I am trying to draw a flag of India and Pakistan tied together. Soldiers from both sides are saluting them. There are no barriers at the border and a temple and a mosque have been built side by side. The people are hugging each other as if they have found their loved ones after 50 years of Independence.' He decided to help her and quickly drew the scene she had described. She was elated with the result, and planted a kiss on his cheek. Then she ran with the drawing directly into the auditorium.

Suddenly he remembered his child, now in a faraway land. She used to come running to him just like this, she would kiss him just like this.

It was almost time for the bombs to explode. But his conscience began to ask prick him. 'How can you be so demonic? How can you end so many angelic lives? Will you ever be able to face your own child? Will you ever be able to rest in peace even after death?' Suddenly, he changed his mind and diffused all the bombs. Then he walked up to that little girl, picked her up, kissed her on the forehead and said, 'Thank you! You have given me the biggest gift in life. You have taught me the lesson of love and peace.' Then he gathered his fellow men and left.

Why not make it a celebration with a purpose, and share a resolution that will help unite our local, national and global communities?

JUST A DROP

Rabia Azam
16 YEARS
KARACHI HIGH SCHOOL, KARACHI

'What next?' I sighed as the morning paper rustled in my hands. I did not open it. Just a quick glance at the front page and I was absorbed in my thoughts.

'What will it be this time—in fact, what CAN it be?' my thudding heart questioned. 'More lives lost in war . . . more murders . . . more children killed . . . deprived of their parents . . . more slaughters . . . more . . . more . . . ENOUGH!'

I could not bear to think—to be precise, I did not know what to think, what to do. Where did I stand amid this evaporation of peace? How could I put an end to it? I sank deeper into the bottomless pit of despair, pushed to the extreme end of helplessness.

I was tired, annoyed at the way the powerful abused their power, frustrated that the innocent were always the victims, exhausted with rights not guaranteed to the rightful and irritated that rules were not rules for the rich, that crimes were not crimes for the powerful, that people in authority could do whatever they wanted—a wrong deed was not wrong if *they* did it!

'But why?' I asked aloud, 'Where is our peace of mind?'

And as I struggled to understand, something clicked into place—the root of it all.

It all begins when people no longer not care about the rights of others. And I do not have to be the president of a country to withhold the rights of those beneath me. At this very minute I could be withholding someone's rights—anybody's. I would not have to go very far but correct myself.

We all need to check ourselves. An employee can be deprived of his rights if the employer abuses his powers. A doctor can withhold a patients right by not giving him or her enough time.

These issues may not be big enough to change the world but they ARE big enough to make a difference—at least some would be granted the peace of mind.

And then, as the saying goes, 'Correct YOURSELF. The world will right itself.'

Alas, I have found the answer to my question.

Now I know what I can do. Passing my message through this story is just a beginning. Let us all be drops in the ocean. No matter how small, every drop does make a difference.

LIBERATION

Abhranil Das
18 YEARS
SOUTH POINT HIGH SCHOOL, CALCUTTA

The warm April wind had been blowing over Celle since the morning. It carried with it the smell of grass, fruits and fragrant German flowers, although it did not need a very discerning sense of smell to also catch the whiff of gunpowder and fire. The wind wandered aimlessly over the fields and roads, swirled about the quaint farmsteads and swooped low over the airstrips, caressing the tarmac with its warm fingers.

Inside the huge black stone building of Bergen-Belsen, no one could tell there was a summer wind blowing outside. The only ones who could were lined up in the courtyard with their belongings, being marched out of the gates. They would have to walk 20 miles to the nearest station. Slowing down or stopping meant a bullet. At the station they would be packed into closed freight cars and be sent off in the suffocating darkness to the nearest death camp.

The greatest venture of human history was on. It was a daunting task, to delete entire races from the face of the planet, but the Nazis had shown that, with careful planning, meticulous control and inflexible ideals, anything was possible. The 'resettlement' in the east had suppressed all uprisings with their extermination camps—factories of death where Jews, Romans, Jehovah's Witnesses and similar filth would be packed in by the thousands from every direction and killed—in gas chambers or burned in pits. The Nazis did not wish this fact to spread, so the ones deported to Auschwitz would be oblivious of their fate until the very last moment.

The ones who survived were those deemed physically fit. Those sent to the right were used as slave labour, 10 to 14 hours a day. Those sent left were requested to put away their belongings and remember where they put them. Their hair would be shaved (for making warm cloth), and they would be led naked into the chambers marked 'Bath'. Sometimes, to keep the panic down, they would be given towels and soap. When they entered, the doors were locked and pellets of Zyklon-B, the killer gas, pumped in through the vents. Those inside could then stop worrying about where they had put their things. The naked corpses were then surveyed for gold teeth or other valuable pickings. The bodies were removed and buried in pits, and the chambers cleaned by the *Sonderkommando,* Jewish prisoners exchanging their labour for a few more months of life. The belongings of the prisoners were redistributed elsewhere in Germany. Of course, accurate knowledge of what went on at these death camps was scarce among the prisoners. What circulated was dark rumours and much-retold accounts of the very few who had been able to escape.

Many refinements of the killing processes had produced large chambers with greater accommodation and more effective gases. All institutions—governmental, commercial, religious—did their own bit to facilitate this process of mass deletion. The result was an efficient, large-scale industrial extermination of the enemies of the Nazi Party. Twenty thousand Jews could now be killed in a day, a huge improvement over the earlier number. The undoable had been done—the Final Solution of the Jewish Question had been achieved.

But support for the great Nazi dream slowly waned. Some felt that the killing of industrially skilled Jews was an economic waste; some others had slightly more humane opinions. The Allies had gained power and were fighting back. Russia, America and Britain had begun to recapture territories from German Occupation, places where unreported tortures and killings had been carried out, villages where the air reeked of burning human fat. Slowly, the full scale of the Nazi project was beginning to unfold. In despair, the Nazis started pulling prisoners from the eastern concentration camps further west, into the heart of Germany. Every day, freight trains brought hundreds from the eastern camps to the extermination centres.

Ernst watched the prisoners from where he stood in the line, clutching his tattered cloth bag with an irrelevant note scribbled by his mother a day before she died, half a cashew for his lunch and two pebbles. Thin, skeletal bodies piled high on both sides of the meandering aisle in which the long deportation line now stood. Every face Ernst looked at betrayed fear. German officers prowled about, occasionally picking out children and old men from the crowd and shooting them. Every shot rang out loud in the still summer afternoon, but it failed to startle even a child such as Ernst—he had got used to it.

Ernst spotted Heinrich in the line ahead, his neighbour, the one who tore his kite and wouldn't stop crying until Ernst made him another. There was Luise, Heinrich's daughter, hiding beneath her mother's cloak. 'She's trying to smuggle her out of here and into a death camp,' thought Ernst. Ernst had spent a lot of his troubled childhood with Luise, running around their crowded ghetto when the German police were not present, climbing roofs and playing war, something for which they were never in short supply of inspiration.

He saw Bernheim further up the line, the young, lively man who always talked about hope, resistance and escape plans. Ernst could still vividly remember his wild, flushed face when he ran into their room one day, clutching a piece of paper. He talked very excitedly about peace and freedom, then laid out the paper for everyone to see. It was a news article in Russian, torn from the previous day's paper:

> SOVIET TROOPS ADVANCE FURTHER. UNEARTH EVIDENCE OF GENOCIDE.
>
> Ravensbrück, April 10, 1945: As of now, the Russian Red Army has progressed further west in the attempt to drive back the Nazis from occupied regions where they had held Jews, gypsies, homosexuals and political opposers captive in different camps. Reporters accompanying our soldiers followed their progress, and have written in about various skeletons in the German closet. The evidence comprises thousands of unburied corpses at the German camps; gas chambers and burning pits, some of which the Germans tried to demolish before leaving. Although it is evident that the Germans tried to mop up operations, the state of the camps conclusively confirms that the prisoners were forced to live in abnormally crowded conditions. Despite liberated survivors being treated at Allied army camps, many have died from a fatal spread of typhus caused by the lack of proper food and sanitation. The colossal mass-elimination of the Jewish population has repeatedly been referred to by the Nazi authorities. As events unfold, we only expect more atrocious evidence

> of the 'Final Solution' to come into full view of the rest of the world.
>
> Air raids by Allied Forces have, in the past few weeks, rendered many railroads defunct, and the primary method of deportation of prisoners to death and concentration camps has been growing increasingly difficult for the Nazis. Still, the Germans are trying their best to transfer the prisoners in eastern camps further west before the Red Army arrives. In spite of their efforts, the situation as of now vouches for a comfortable progress for the Allied troops into the west. Sources state that the liberation of prisoners from the remaining death and concentration camps is only a matter of weeks, after which the generals behind the Final Solution will be tried in courts of law.

'Look, look!' Bernheim stabbed his finger at the paper with burning eyes, his thin, starving face flushed and sweaty, the veins pulsing at his temples. 'I told you! I told you to keep your hopes up and drag on for a few more days. Here they are! Here they are at last and the war is over, everyone! Now it's just a matter of not getting deported west before they arrive. We'll live! We'll live, everyone, and they'll let us out and we can have food and bathing water again, and freedom and peace!'

Bernheim hadn't been lucky enough to escape deportation. He was standing in the grounds, sweating and fidgety, as the long line started to move slowly out of the gates. His last hopes of survival had turned to dust.

Ernst's eyes hovered over to Officer Franz Meyer, a young German, possibly in his twenties, patrolling the line, occasionally prodding a prisoner with the end of his rifle. This was the last time Ernst would see him. The first had been on the day of their arrival at Bergen-Belsen. Some time after 13 of them had been shoved into a tiny room with one window, and low murmurs had begun to break out in the stuffy silence, that there was a loud banging on the door and a gruff voice ordered them in German to shut up or be shot.

Every voice in the room died down at once. Only a baby cried loudly. The mother tried her best to stop her child, looking helplessly at the other faces in the shadows. The door was banged on again. Ernst was at the other end of the room. He never knew what happened but the crying stopped abruptly and was replaced by the mother's quiet sobs.

Suddenly, the door was flung open to reveal an officer, silhouetted against a patch of blinding daylight. Behind him stood a second officer, leaner and younger, squinting into the darkness of the room. The first officer bellowed loudly in German—that same gruff voice—demanding to know who had made the noise. The mother put her baby in someone else's arms and stood up. The officer ordered her to step outside. She began to cry, but obeyed. The officer aimed his rifle at the centre of her forehead and shot once. She fell, the blood slowly pooling in a halo around her head. The younger officer stared at her body for a few moments, then shut the door.

In the darkness of their room, the baby was found to be dead. Its frightened mother had choked it into silence.

The day after, Ernst was summoned by the young officer after roll-call. As he walked up to him, he felt a mad urge to run away, to shout for his parents, but then he remembered they were long dead,. That memory made him stand frozen in front of the lean, fair man.

The officer looked at Ernst for a few seconds, then asked, '*Was ist dein name*?'

An innocent question, but it caused an amazing number of visions in Ernst's head: the officer noting it down, making sure he was selected for the deportation to the west, the long, frozen walk to the station across the dirty snow, the dark, packed freight compartment where many died, the death camp, the gas chamber, the gas vents, pain, darkness.

'Ernst, Sir. *Mein name ist Ernst Gruber*.'

He surveyed Ernst with his cold steely eyes for a little longer, then shuffled in the pocket of his uniform. He produced a black cloth bag, took a cashew nut from it and held it out to him. Ernst looked up at him in fear. The officer's eyes were still grey and cold, but he nodded once. Ernst took the offering and looked up again. With the same impassive expression, Officer Meyer said in German, 'Run.'

Ernst had heard about this a lot, even seen it once from the window of his room in the ghetto. A truck of German soldiers had arrived late one night and marched a number of Jews out into the middle of the road. An officer had said, 'Run.' All the Jews had run, except one. Then the Germans shot them in the back. When the sound of gunfire faded away, and the night grew quiet again, the officer had looked down and smiled at the one Jew still standing.

'You didn't run. Good.'

The man smiled back with terrified eyes.

The soldiers got into their truck. As it drew away, the officer leaned out and shot him. The Jew fell dead, his hands clasped in mute surrender.

That vision came whirling back to Ernst. He looked up once at the cold, unfeeling eyes of the officer, then turned and ran like a hare, his heart thudding in his ears.

There were no shots.

The day after, Officer Meyer came and took Ernst out of the room. This time Ernst knew he was done for. No German ever did anything good for a Jew. He had been foolish to imagine that the matter was over, that he had been able to escape from a German officer.

Officer Meyer told Ernst his name, gave him a cashew nut and ordered him to run.

There were no shots.

For a week this continued, until Ernst slowly developed an inexplicable trust in him and realized he would not shoot. Why he chose to trust a German officer he did not know. Perhaps because he had run out of everything else in which to trust.

Today was Ernst's eighth day in Bergen-Belsen, and he was standing in the line to be deported west, fully aware that children and old men were usually, although not always, dragged out of the line and killed on the spot before the walk began.

The other older officer was present and now approached Heinrich's wife. He had noticed the girl she was trying to conceal with her cloak. He grabbed her thin arms and yanked her out of the line. The mother fell to her knees, crying, begging, imploring. The officer held his rifle to her head and drawled, 'If you don't want to die too, get back in line.' The mother got up, sobbing, and returned slowly to the line as Luise stared at her, her eyes wide with disbelief.

Then the officer smiled at Luise and shot her in the chest. Her frail body crumpled without a sound.

Something inside Ernst squeezed his soul into a tight ball. Luise. Next-door Luise. Happiness, sunshine, laughter. His only friend. Now a lump of skin, bones and rags, lying in the dust.

The officer stepped over her body and looked down the line. His eyes stopped at Ernst. The corners of his mouth twitched in satisfaction. Ernst's heart began to pound.

Suddenly, something hard and cold pressed into the back of his neck. He looked up to see Officer Meyer and his rifle. Meyer smiled at the other officer, 'Relax, Otto. I'll take it from here. You go see that side.'

Otto nodded, gave Ernst a menacing look and left. 'Give him something he'll remember, Franz,' he said as he strolled away.

Ernst looked up into the cold grey eyes of Officer Meyer. He was grabbed and pulled out of the line, the rifle still held to the back of his head. 'Walk.' Ernst put his hands up and obeyed. They rounded a corner where there were no patrolling officers and from where the line of prisoners were no longer in sight.

'Stop,' said Officer Meyer. 'Turn around.'

Ernst turned, his hands still in the air. The long black nozzle of the rifle pointed between his eyes. He looked into its darkness, then up at the officer. No German soldier ever did anything good for a Jew.

Officer Meyer looked at him coldly for a second—the huge, unfeeling black nozzle swaying in front of Ernst's eyes—then said, 'Run.'

Ernst turned and ran, clutching his tattered bag close to his body, his heart beating louder than the clatter of his footsteps. He felt the dirty stone walls of the camp sliding away from him, the ground slipping beneath his feet.

There were no shots. Ernst stormed into the room, breathless. Every eye in the group stared at him in mute surprise. He stood there, panting, speechless. Looking at the faces.

A few more hours of life.

After answering the eager queries about his return, all of which were met with disbelief, Ernst sat down and opened his bag. Looking around to see if anyone was watching, he quickly slipped the cashew nut into his mouth. He was still chewing, long after the nut had been eaten, rolling around the inside of his head its exquisite taste, when there were a couple of shots outside and voices shouting in a language he did not know.

Ernst was so used to hearing gunshot that he could immediately tell that this was of a different kind. Different gun, different bullets.

He ran to the window before anyone else. The whole room crowded around him and peered out.

A number of armed men in a different uniform were running through the courtyard. A few of them stopped the deportation line walking out of the gates. Some German officers were lying dead, along with the one that killed Luise. The prisoners were trembling in fear. Ernst saw another troop of these soldiers run to the back of the camp. There were repeated gunshots. Five new. One old. Then voices, shouting—some in German, some in a new language.

There was a sudden banging on the door.

Everyone in the room froze. They could hear the sound of running boots outside. The banging again, and a voice.

'We are British. We have come to save you. We are going to open the door—don't be afraid. We have come to rescue you.' Once in the foreign tongue, again in halting German.

Then the door was opened by a soldier. He stared wide-eyed for a few seconds, taking in the condition of the room and its inhabitants, then said in faltering German, 'Get out. You're free. You're going to an army camp with us for food and medicine.'

A few seconds of stunned silence, then it was as if the whole room woke up as a single being. The murmurs grew to shouting and cheering, and they trooped out and joined the other streams of half-naked starving men, women and children running out of their dark prisons. Everyone was stunned, struggling to absorb the shock of this new reality.

Ernst skipped down the stairs, pushing through the crowds. All around him he could hear commands being shouted in broken German. When he reached the courtyard, he saw pools of blood and the bodies of German officers lying everywhere. Some knelt beside a wall while a British soldier stood guard. So some were still alive, thought Ernst, running through the chaos. He reached the gate. And saw.

Officer Meyer's body lay face up and spread-eagled, his steel grey eyes looking up at the summer sky. There was blood on his chest, and bootmarks.

As Ernst stood looking at him, Officer Meyer's impassive voice sounded softly inside his head, 'Run.'

Ernst knelt down beside the body. He did not feel like crying. He did not feel like anything. He looked around once. No one was looking this way. He slipped a hand inside a blood-smeared pocket and drew out the black cloth bag of cashews.

Then he ran out of the gates, pushing through the line being led through the fields by the British soldiers. He ran to the middle of the field, panting heavily. He had eaten almost nothing in the past few days, but he wouldn't touch the nuts.

As he looked around, the rough ground beneath his bare feet, the warm summer breeze, the clear wide sky above his head—all these filtered slowly back into his consciousness. He breathed in the smell of fire, gunpowder and wild German flowers. Peace, freedom. What would life be like, now?

He looked back at the camp. For the first time, the dark, inflexible stone walls of Bergen-Belsen failed to intimidate him. They only filled him with a sharp and painful burst of sadness. Luise, friend through so many times. The sunshine and happiness in his childhood full of squalor and hate. Ernst stared at the iron gates. They seemed to be calling him back. The dark rooms, the long roll-calls under the blazing sun, the alleys of the dead, the incessant shooting . . .

Ernst tore himself from his thoughts and looked back at the glittering blue sky and the glowing summer fields through which the line of prisoners progressed. And, very slowly, a vision rose before his eyes. Officer Meyer, and his cold grey eyes that never betrayed any emotion. The blue summer sky in his eyes, and the bootmarks on his chest. 'Run,' he said to Ernst, clear and gentle, motioning forward.

Ernst clasped the bag of cashew nuts tighter in his hand, gathered all the strength and hope he had left, and started running towards the long line walking out of the gates.

NOT OUR PROBLEM

Nikunja Gupta
15 YEARS
SPRINGDALES SCHOOL, NEW DELHI

It was the time of ancient kings and queens. Of immense palaces. And the rule of one king and his favourites. King Theophalis was the great heir of a great country. An arrogant man, he was cruel and mean to those who he regarded as lesser men.

It was a hot summer afternoon and Theophalis was with his friend, also a distinguished member of his court. They were seated beside the window of the Great Hall, enjoying a delicious meal of fruits, bread and honey. Immersed in court talk, they glanced from time to time out of the window and at the street below.

Theophalis, a large man with a heavy paunch, lay comfortably against a cushion on the silk sofa, an elbow on the window sill. As he bit into his honey sandwich, a drop of honey fell on the sill. The king was much more interested in his comfort and noticed nothing. However, the sight of the yellow drop against the clean window made his friend uneasy and he made a move to wipe it. Theophalis, unconcerned, said, 'Never mind. It's not our problem. The servants can clean it.'

The two men continued their conversation. Meanwhile, the drop of honey, eager for some movement, began to run down the window, leaving behind a long, sticky, yellow stain, and finally fell on the street below, near a mosquito buzzing around a lamp. The mosquito was restless and sniffing around eagerly when it came across the drop of honey. Delighted, it began its supper.

Just then, a lizard, merrily slithering along on the road, noticed the feasting mosquito. She pounced on him and swallowed him in one gulp. It could well have continued its game of jumping jack but fortune does not always lie in the hands (or paws) of all!

Meanwhile, a handsome black tomcat, sitting on a wall, raised its 20 claws and struck the tiny lizard. The reptile squeezed out of the cat's clutches. But the cat, not in the mood to accept defeat, ran after it. Suddenly, from behind a bush, emerged the little kitty's best friend, a big golden Labrador.

Smelling a race in progress, it too joined in and fell upon the cat in a trice. An enormous fight between the two animals broke out, creating a loud combination of meows and barks.

This caused our two other characters, Theophalis and his friend, to once again look out of the window. The friend, a lover of animals, wanted to stop the fight and asked the king to send someone over. However, the king couldn't be bothered with such small things, and said, 'Never mind. It's not our problem. The people down there can fix it.'

Their lunch continued and so did the fight between the cat and the dog. Soon their owners, missing their pets, came calling for them. But the cat was so angry that she would not stop scratching the dog. The dog, thrilled at the chance of strangling the cat, would not give up either.

The cat's owner, a tall man with a long beard, started to shoo off the dog with a stick. The owner of the dog, a fat man, began chasing the cat with his cane. Both men, overlooking the faults of their respective pets (about which they did not know much), began to blame and hit the other's, causing such a ruckus that several onlookers stopped and tried to investigate the cause of the commotion.

The king and his friend, halfway through their custard pies, looked down from the window again. Seeing the two men and their animals fighting, the friend said, 'There are two men having a quarrel. Shall we send someone to sort it out?' To which the king replied lazily, 'Never mind. It's not our problem. They're grown-ups. They'll stop soon.'

But they did not stop. Rather, the encounter now embarked on a discussion of the ways in which each pet had been bred and brought up. Friends and companions as well as local residents joined in. After a few minutes, there were two separate groups of people fighting. Accusations drifted away from the pets and began to focus on the owners.

The king and his friend began an easy debate on what the reason could be. The king, however, was not bothered in the least. Every time his friend suggested looking into the matter, he repeated, 'Never mind. It's not our problem. They can solve it themselves.'

In the meantime, a few soldiers happened to be passing by. They noticed the fight and tried to break it up. When they heard the cause (which every one had lost track of), they split up between the two groups depending on their personal opinions, and joined in the fray. With soldiers involved, the fight escalated to an alarming level and spread through the city. Streets were in flames, houses burned down, many people died. Even the king's palace was stoned to the ground.

After a few months, when the king and his friend were surveying the ruins, the king said, ashamed, 'Perhaps it was our problem our after all!'

PEACE, A MYTH

Ananya Dixit
17 YEARS
SOUTH POINT HIGH SCHOOL, CALCUTTA

The river Banak, lifeline of the Manipuri district of Adubi, the one closest to Nagaland, was meandering cheerfully down the rugged valley. It cackled joyously, like an ecstatic child who has just taken his first few faltering steps. The crystal-clear water reflected the sun's rays and sparkled like a brilliantly cut diamond. In the background, one could see Mt Japvo, shrouded in snow, exuding pride and power, looking over Adubi like a guardian. The valley was dotted with tall pines and conifers, their leaves bright green, whispering exotic verses as the cool and crisp morning breeze swished past them. Somewhere, someone played a soft tune on a flute. The sound floated through the entire valley.

The fluteplayer could be spotted easily, like a blot marring the perfection of the entire scene. Shabby and doleful, he wore faded brown corduroy pants and a woollen jacket that seemed to consist entirely of patches. His shoes could betray him at any moment, and the cap on his long hair was in tatters. The only sign of gaiety in his entire forlorn demeanour could be found in his eyes, which shone with a merry glint. Sunk into their sockets and surrounded by wrinkles, his eyes nevertheless had a look in them that was both as innocent as a baby and as playful as a colt. He appeared to be in a trance. Suddenly, a rugged voice called out: 'Zoramthangi, look! The Sahibs have given the money.'

'Uh?! Oh, yes! The money. How much?'

'*Bas,* 50 rupees. Each. These *firangs* are getting miserly.'

'Why? Fifty's ok, Magong!'

'You never think of money. All is OK for YOU but . . . what were you thinking of sitting here?'

'See the river Banak? There was a day when even I was like her. Young, Energetic . . . '

'Oh, yes! . . . Come, let's go. I've fished out 'nother group of tourists. Come!'

Zoram and Magong were *sherpas*—porters. They carried luggage uphill for the tourists, trekkers, forest officers and army jawans. Their condition was worse than that of the daily wage-earners. Their earnings were irregular and dismally low and they faced great difficulties in maintaining a family, but still they did. These days, Zoram was very apprehensive about the future. He was growing older and slowly lacked the power and energy to work for hours at length. He had to stop every 20 steps to catch his breath—but he was the sole bread earner of the family. What would become of his wife, his daughter and his son when he was no longer able to work? Amid these anxieties, his pillar of strength was his son, Devang. Zoram had saved as much as he could from his meagre income and paid for his son's education.

Devang was a good student, and now studying engineering at a college in Imphal. He was an energetic youth with progressive thoughts. He believed that the new generation was capable of creating an Utopia, where liberty, equality and peace would prevail. He was into student politics and believed that that would lead to his eventual attempt at national leadership. He was the secretary of the students' union and a firm believer in activism.

Those were the days when relations between Manipur and Nagaland had turned sour. The Manipuri areas adjacent to Nagaland's borders were largely inhabited by tribes originally belonging to Nagaland but who had settled in Manipur long ago. (Adubi was one such.) The Nagas now wanted these areas to be included within their state borders. As expected, the Manipuris vehemently protested. The situation was turning explosive and, every now and then, groups from both states clashed violently. The peace and tranquility of the serene hillside were lost. The central government paid no heed for it was busy making peace with Pakistan.

Devang was also a part of this. He would organize rallies and marches and deliver dynamic speeches and try to build general consensus in his favour. He was extremely popular with the common people who had started imagining him as their new leader, one who would be true to his promises. This fame and recognition was earning him enemies too, as the local political leaders could not bear to see people swooning over a young student instead of them. They conspired against Devang and coaxed an opposing student leader into beginning on a parallel movement. But the plan met with no success.

In pursuit of the anti-Naga movement, Devang visited Adubi, his home. He met Zoram after two years and Zoram's eyes welled up with tears at the meeting. Devang enthralled the Adubi residents with his views and witty speeches. Zoram understood very little of what Devang said but his chest swelled with pride whenever words of wisdom issued from Devang's mouth. Zoram—now recognized as Devang's father—was bestowed with additional respect. All this made Zoram live the dream he had woven around Devang. But, alas, Zoram forgot that dreams are short-lived.

The political leaders on both sides, striving to oust Devang from the place he had carved for himself, now approached him with a plan—he should threaten to immolate himself if the Central Government did not look into the matter. According to them, the government would most definitely take steps to save face and peace would be restored immediately. Devang, an innocent, was immediately taken with the idea. He had no clue what the lust for power could do to the minds of men. An Utopian, he readily fell for their suggestion, completely unaware that these power-hungry people were using a concept as holy as peace to serve their selfish interests.

Devang thus announced his intention to self-immolate much to the horror of everyone. Zoram was shocked and desperately tried to stop Devang from this dangerous stint, but Devang was sure his political mentors would take care of everything.

Zoram doubled his visits to the church and lived in horror of the day. On that fateful day, Devang positioned himself in the local football stadium as many anxious eyes watched on. He announced that he would put an end to his life if the government did not act immediately. Some people in the crowd thought he was extremely heroic and patriotic while others thought he was wasting his life. Zoram sat in a corner, thumbing a rosary.

Devang, meanwhile, was addressing the gathering. 'Brothers and sisters, I do not fear my death. I will never let our land go to the Nagas. If my death can sort this problem, then let it be so!' Pouring kerosene all over himself, he waited for his mentors to say something and happy with the success of their plan.

When suddenly . . .

The crowd roared. Devang was engulfed in flames—shouting and running helter skelter for help. One of the leaders' goons had thrown a lighted match at him. The leaders promptly began speeches lauding Devang's courage and declared him a martyr. Zoram was struggling to free himself from the grasp of his friends, longing to save his son. But to no avail. Devang succumbed. He succumbed to deceit, to foul intentions, to *peace*.

After two days, the Centre formed a committee comprising the minister of state, the principal secretary and six other officials to look into the matter and submit a report within six months. A peace accord between the two states was quickly prepared, to be signed by the chief ministers of both states.

The ministers met in a hotel. Handshakes, music and chatter filled the air. Zoram meanwhile was at the cemetery, at Devang's grave, silent and lost. The tears of a lonely father, bereft of his dearest son, narrate the tale of grief and deceit. The peace accord was signed and celebrations broke out. The sun set on the western horizon, Zoram's 'son' was set aflame a few days ago. With quivering hands, Zoram planted a rose bulb on Devang's grave. A muffled sob breaks out, and the sound of it looms over the entire valley, the now peaceful valley. Peace was at last restored but at a heavy price. And only Zoram bore the price. He lost a son whom he held in high esteem, whom he loved more than himself. He lost the apple of his eye to bring peace to the state but this *peace* has shattered him to *pieces*. Zoram returned home with heavy steps, but with a heavier heart. The peaceful surroundings appeared monstrous to him. He was never going to believe in peace again. Peace was a myth, a treacherous myth.

PEACE IN THE FAST LANE

Sayan Ray
16 YEARS
SOUTH POINT HIGH SCHOOL, CALCUTTA

AUTHOR'S NOTE

Formula One is one of the most demanding versions of motorsport. It requires excellent driving skills, a steady head, high levels of fitness and loads of concentration. A total of 20 to 22 cars race around a circuit to complete a minimum of 50 to 70 laps. The technicalities are quite complicated. However, it should be mentioned that, unlike street cars, Formula One cars are much, much faster and extremely aerodynamically designed. The steering wheel is in the shape of a rectangle with an array of controls on it, including the gears, an automatic start button and a digital speedometer. There is also a radio located in the cockpit which helps the driver to continuously interact with the team members, including the technical director who calls all the shots. Before the race, the cars go through a 'warm-up lap' after which they line up once more and the race begins. An A1 Grand Prix car is pretty similar.

Imola is home to the Enzo and Dino Autodrome. This race circuit is one of the most demanding of its kind and possibly the most dangerous, having witnessed the deaths of two promising Formula One drivers. But it has defied logic and continued to host races when many people said it could not.

'Accidents in the fast lane are part and parcel of the game,' the head of the Formula One governing body had once remarked. Thus, Imola was now hosting the third round of the A1 Grand Prix, a championship involving pace drivers from all over the globe, representing their respective countries in cars that were similar save their set-up and colours. One such driver is currently roaming between the cars, taking a close look at all of them. Like the other drivers, he is ambitious, urged on by a desire to win. And his passion for racing is possibly second to none. He has rebelled against his parents, especially his father, to be here.

'Why?' his father had asked. 'Why not an engineer, a software analyst or a lawyer?' It was his grandfather, a former rally driver, who recognized his talent and who urged his parents to let the boy pursue his dreams. He had bought him a go-kart when he was 10, and the full kit. Then trained him, day after day, night after night. The boy's name is Aryan Khan. Tall, muscular, with a pair of cobalt blue eyes and a mass of neatly combed dark hair, he could have been quite a hit in Tinseltown. Luckily for Indian motorsport, this exceptionally talented driver chose otherwise. Khan rose through the ranks, from go-karting to Formula Renault to the A1 Grand Prix and was now knocking on the doors of the big game—Formula One, where no one but the very best can compete or even dream to compete. But his road to success had been bumpy—a lack of sponsors, injuries, accidents. Aryan had seen it all.

It seems only yesterday that he got a call from top man of Indian motorsport. 'Would you like to represent India in the A1 Grand Prix?' Like? He was delighted. He packed his bags and soon, landed with the entire team at Sylverstone for the first race. He made it to tenth place—his best so far—but he had to do better. His sponsors called him two days before the fourth round: 'Finish in the top five or do the next round without us.'

Aryan knows he won't be able to go to Spain without his sponsors. Thus, when he gets to his position on the grid (twentieth), he is a trifle nervous. It'll be quite a job getting up to fifth from here. As Aryan mulls the task before him, someone bumps into him, someone short and muscular. It is Alam Qureshi, the ace Pakistani driver who starts just behind him. Friends since their go-karting days, they have always shared a common bond—racing, like Ayrton Senna (a common idol). It was Senna who had been the most sought-after driver of his era but his bright career had been cut short by a terrible accident on this same circuit.

'It's going to rain', said Qureshi and added, jokingly, 'Mate, go a bit easy on the race. I'm right behind you.'

'You know I'll never do that,' replied Aryan, smiling. 'May the best man win.'

'You—' said Alam, and they shook hands.

Five minutes later, they are in their cars. After the warm-up lap, they line up once more. The lights glow red, then green. Aryan presses the kick-start button and the orange and green car surges forward. Simultaneously, a thin rain begins to fall. As the car surges ahead, Aryan feels as if his soul has a new set of wings. This is where he belongs. A race car has never been just a race car for Aryan, it has been a home away from home. Aryan is already in fourteenth place. And, amazingly, Qureshi is right behind him.

'Pits, Aryan!' shouts the technical director, Mike, over the radio. After a change of tyres, he rejoins the race and, to his good fortune, maintains his position. Already the circuit has turned dangerously slippery because of the rain; four cars, from Germany, England, France and Mexico, have crashed out. But Aryan has no problem—he always liked driving in the rain. He realizes he is in tenth place because of the crashes. Five more, he tells himself. Come on! The car before him skids off into the pit wall. Aryan is now at ninth. He knows Qureshi is still behind him but going rather slow.

'Never liked the rain, did you,' thinks Aryan and smiles inside his helmet. Then, amazingly, he manages to overtake a couple of cars and moves into seventh place. He is informed over the radio that only eight cars are left. The one in front of him blows its engine and is forced to retire. Aryan now has the remaining Mexican driver within his sights. In the next lap, Aryan overtakes him to come up to fifth. 'All right! Now can we just finish the race?' Aryan says aloud.

Suddenly Mike's voice comes through the radio. 'Aryan, move aside, let Qureshi go.'

'Mike, you okay?' asks Aryan, laughing. 'Told you not to have that can of beer before the race.'

'Aryan, I'm serious. The order's from the Prime Minister of India. He's told the Pakistani leader that he'll request his chap to let the Pakistani one go ahead. If he finishes in a respectable position, it will go a long way to promote Pakistani motorsport as well as strengthen ties between the two countries. I know this means a lot to you but if you don't do this, we may not be in Spain this time next week.'

Aryan nearly crashes his car into the pit wall. 'Let Qureshi go? Pakistani motorsport? Peace between India and Pakistan?'

'He'll block the funds, dammit! Please, for your country's sake—'

'For my Prime Minister's sake, isn't it? He wants to show us he's doing something for peace. Another term, another meeting with the Pakistani leader. All that talk amounting to nothing. Why? Why's it always me?' Aryan angrily thrusts the car forward, pulling away from the struggling Qureshi.

For the first time, Aryan was enjoying life, a life that had so far always plucked away his every happiness, that had not allowed him to cry when he wanted to, a life that found great joy in snatching away his sources of gladness—his brother had succumbed to cancer last year, his grandfather, his friend, philosopher and guide, had died a week ago. Aryan had never known the meaning of 'peace'. To him it had always been an abstract noun. Peace? What the hell is that? He knew if he backed off now he would lose his position as well as any chance of retaining his sponsors. He wouldn't be going to Spain nor sit in a race car again. His father would make sure of that.

'Finish the next race and come back. You're going to New York to do an MBA,' he had said on the phone last night. His life hit back at him once more. Aryan was tired of this life. He shut off the radio, knowing he couldn't put Mike's career in danger. Mike had been recruited to help the team out and had greatly improved his handling of the car. He now approached the corner where his idol, Ayrton Senna, had gone straight off and smashed into the tyre wall and died a horrific death. Suddenly the idea hit Aryan. It was so simple. He had found a way to establish national peace as well as finally give up on this miserable life of his.

He switched the radio back on.

'Mike, I want to thank you for everything you've done for us.

The car feels great—just the suspension needs to be a bit lighter.' Before Mike realized anything, Aryan switched the radio off.

'Next lap,' he told himself. A few seconds later he neared the historic bend. Suddenly he felt the spirit of Senna within him and his hands grew firm. His visor down, no one saw his closed eyes, his lips moving in a final prayer, his grandfather's face and his go-karting days flashing before his mind's eye, a tear trickling down his cheek—

SCREEEEECH!

Aryan's eyes open just in time to see a green car pass in front of him, lose control and head for the gravel.

Aryan pulled out of the dive straight away. Dammit!

He switched the radio back on.

'Mike, what the hell just happened?'

'Qureshi tried to sneak in front and lost control. He's currently scrambling out of his car which you stuck in the gravel. So you won't have to back off, mate. Put your head down and finish the bloody race!'

That is exactly what Aryan does. And overtakes two more cars to finish third. But he doesn't jump or cry out in joy when he gets out of his car. Just mechanically hugs a few of his mates and staff. Puts down his helmet which basks in the sun that has finally broken through the dark clouds. Something just doesn't fit. Qureshi tried to overtake him? He never tried to, the whole race. Moreover he went off at right angles. It didn't even seem like he was trying to move the car's nose in.

Aryan walked across to the Pakistani garage, which is oddly deserted save for Qureshi, sitting on a stack of Michelin tyres. Qureshi looks cool for a man who's just blown a chance to finish in the top five. He's plugged into his iPod and munching a bar of chocolate.

'What did you just do?' Aryan asked.

'Finished a can of Coke,' said Qureshi, smiling.

'Cut it out! You know what I mean.'

'Okay! I just went off the road to save the life of an Indian who was prepared to say bon voyage to a highly successful life just because some damn Prime Ministers wanted to fix the race for the sake of peace. Peace? You call this peace? Peace that is ready to sacrifice the life of a promising driver just for the sake of publicity? You know Aryan, the day India and Pakistan come together will be when they finally manage to understand each other's interests, not question each ones ideas and moves. When they learn to live like respectful neighbours. Pakistani motor-sport will improve not when a certain Alam Qureshi finishes in the top five but when several Aryan Khans emerge.'

Aryan was dumbfounded. 'How the hell did you—'

'Know all this? It was Mike. He got hold of me.'

'But how did you know, I was going to—'

'Don't be silly, Aryan, I saw you straightening the nose, the wheels were at right angles directly in line with the corner where Senna crashed. Remember when we were having a stroll around this circuit last night? You remarked how nice it would be to die in a racing car, on this circuit, at this very corner, when the time comes? I'm not a fool.'

'But what about you, won't you—'

'Relax, no need to worry about me. I'll be fine. Anyway, enjoy the moment, it's your hour.'

Aryan turned around, then stopped and turned around to face Qureshi once more. Qureshi's deep black eyes stared back. 'I saved not only a great driver, a great man and a great Indian but also a great friend. Dammit—who's going to beat me in the 100-metre race, who's going to beat me in the freestyle fights and who's going to teach me the art of balancing speed and precision?!'

They hugged each other—an Indian driver hugged a Pakistani driver, an Indian hugged a Pakistani. Not just for show, not because of the cars flashing in the background, but because they were the greatest of friends.

PEACE LIES IN PIECES

Vinayak Shukl
15 YEARS
SPRINGDALES SCHOOL, NEW DELHI

'Aamir,' said Ritika, handing her brother a cutting from a Delhi morning paper dated 20 December, 'Just read this about children's toys, please. It brings out some of your ideas about influences in upbringing.'

'In the view of the National Peace Council,' read the extract, 'there are grave objections to presenting our children with regiments of fighting men, batteries of guns and squadrons of fighter jets. Boys, the Council admits, naturally love fighting and everything else related to war. But that is no reason for encouraging their primitive instincts. At the forthcoming 'Peace Toys' exhibition at the Centre for Peace, the Peace Council will present alternative suggestions to parents.'

'Certainly an interesting and well-meaning idea', said Aamir. 'Whether it will succeed and can be practised—'

‘We must try,’ interrupted his sister. ‘In any case, we’re going to Mumbai this Christmas, and you always bring the boys toys. It’ll be an excellent opportunity for you to try the new experiment. Buy only those toys that have a special bearing on civilian life in its more peaceful aspects. I’ll expect your Christmas gifts to give quite a new direction to the children’s minds. Rohan isn’t eleven yet, and Akshay’s only nine-and-a-half. They’re really at a most impressionable age.’

On Christmas Eve, Aamir unpacked a large red cardboard box under the expectant eyes of his nephews. ‘It must be the new robo-soldiers,’ exclaimed Rohan, ‘with missiles mounted on their backs and a pistol in each hand.’

A bunch of paper shavings was the first thing that met their eye when the lid was removed—the most exciting toys always began like that. Aamir delved in and drew out a square and rather plain building.

‘It’s a fort with no windows or doors to allow bullets to enter. What an awesome piece of engineering!’ exclaimed Akshay, ready to put his hands on the new toy.

‘It’s a municipal dustbin,’ observed Aamir, ‘All the refuse and litter of a town is collected here instead of lying about and injuring the health of the citizens.’

In an atmosphere brittle with dashed hopes, Aamir took out a little lead figure of a man in black clothes.

'This,' he said, 'is a distinguished civilian, Dr Chandra.'

Akshay grunted—there was no accounting for taste.

The toys kept coming—but not a single gun emerged. This was the worst Christmas gift the boys had ever received. Soon, a strange looking box made its appearance.

'This box with a slit is a ballot-box. Votes are put into it at election times.'

'What is put into it at other times?' asked Rohan.

'Nothing. And here are some tools of industry—a wheelbarrow and a hoe, and I think this vehicle is used to clean roads. This seems to be another municipal dustbin—no, it's a model of a school of art and public library.'

'Are we to play with these silly figures?' asked Rohan.

'Of course!' said Aamir, 'These are toys. You're meant to play with them!'

'How?'

'You can make two toys contest a seat in Parliament,' said Aamir, 'and have an election—'

'With fights, lies and broken heads!' exclaimed Rohan.

'With noses bleeding and everybody drunk and out of control!' echoed Akshay.

'Nothing of the kind,' said Aamir, 'Votes will be put in the ballot-box, and the mayor will count them and announce the winner. This is a jolly good game for you boys to play. I never had such toys when I was young.'

'I don't think we'll play with them just now,' said Rohan, with a total absence of enthusiasm. 'I think perhaps we ought to do a little of our holiday tasks. It's Math this time. We've got to learn up something about algebra.'

After a while, Aamir thought it was time to go to their room, and see how they were getting on with their 'peace' toys. As he stood outside the door, he could hear Rohan's high-pitched voice talking excitedly and Akshay interrupting with helpful suggestions whenever he got an opportunity.

Peeping in, Aamir noticed that the municipal dustbin had been mercilessly pierced to look like the muzzles of imaginary cannons. Dr Chandra had been dipped in red ink, and apparently stood for General Singh.

'The General orders his troops to surround the school and seize the terrorists.'

'"I'll never let you go," says the terrorist, "Never" and stabs General Singh through the heart.'

'He's bleeding horribly,' exclaimed Akshay, splashing more red ink over the facade of the school building.

'The soldier's rush into the school to avenge the General's death. A score of children are killed'—the excitement was mounting, and Akshay emptied the remainder of the red ink over the school—'and the surviving 500 are dragged off to shelters. "We have lost the General," cries another soldier, "but we do not go back empty-handed. All the terrorists have been destroyed." '

Aamir quietly stole away from the room, and sought out his sister.

'Ritika—'

'Yes?'

'I think we underestimated the kids. Our experiment has failed. Peace now lies in pieces.'

There was nothing else to be said.

THE DEATH OF WINTER

Kashmira Majumdar
15 YEARS
MODERN HIGH SCHOOL FOR GIRLS, CALCUTTA

'And after many a summer dies the swan; me only cruel immortality consumes . . .'

Shadrach was reading poetry in the empty carriage, the train rattling over the tracks through the barren countryside, ravaged by a war no one was glad to survive.

It was still morning, the hours slowly creeping past dawn. Farouk was fumbling with a tall steel thermos and some plastic cups, trying to pour coffee, and Antar, their other and last travelling companion, had his beaky nose pressed flat against the window, his eyes greedily swallowing the vistas rushing past.

Perhaps the other carriages were empty, perhaps they were littered with men—the three of them didn't know. They were aboard an illegal carriage. While the war was on, the trains were not allowed to take soldiers out of the country. Not deserters, certainly.

Three men, their hands joined in sin. It was a romantic way of looking at a most unromantic thing. They were not honourable men but cowards. Running away from a carnage they could not bear to aggravate, could not face.

They were men robbed of hope, abandoned by God, left to strive for their survival in the wilderness. For them, the war was over.

They were leaving, to start afresh.

There was nothing comforting about Tennyson's verses as Shadrach read them out, slowly but appreciatively, from the upper berth, lean, his strong legs stretched out before him. How Antar resented him for being able to walk.

Farouk handed them their coffee—their breakfast. All their rations had been exhausted during the unending journey from the battlefield to the first train they could stagger into. The train juddered over the tracks. The world outside the window was stripped of vegetation, reduced to flat rolling fields. A tree stood crookedly in the distance, its branches waving.

The train banked into a dirty, deserted station with a screech and a final shudder set the men lurching on their feet.

They had no bags. Only the rifles slung over their shoulders and their last belt of ammunition.

One by one, they leapt down onto the platform. Leaving the train seemed to them a strangely final act. Antar had to use the footboard—he hobbled heavily on one leg because shrapnel had nearly taken off the other.

There was a town, a mile east of the station. It said so on the metal sign hammered against a wall. There was no one at the ticket counter, no one on the benches, waiting, not even a beggar.

The sign said they were in the foothills of Assam. They had crossed the border into India sometime the day before but none of them had been awake long enough to notice. Fainting from hunger, they'd spent the journey sleeping, taking turns, one by one, to stay awake, on guard.

It was an unnamed mining town, the sign said. And offered no more information.

For the three of them, it was the ideal haven. *No one would find them there*.

Under the heat of a fading Indian summer, the three men in their muddied camouflage, raked with grime and sweat, looked undeniably suspicious, and it was left to Farouk to invent convincing lies and save their skins.

They had found bowls of scrap to eat at a tumbledown roadside eatery, where the benches groaned under their weight and the flies buzzed about the rafters clouded with cobwebs. The proprietor—the lone man in the small establishment—wandered off somewhere, but reappeared soon enough, flanked by so many of the townsfolk that cold fingers of fear stroked Shadrach's spine.

'Who're you?'

Those two words sparked off a volley of questions and muttering. About 20 people crowded around the entrance and exit, effectively trapping the three men. Most of them were armed with tall sticks, and one of them was fingering a rusty pistol.

Under the table, two pairs of feet nudged Farouk's boots. He stood up, and opened his mouth with its silver tongue.

He invented their names and made them out to be three strangers who'd met on the road—Antar, a soldier returned from the front on account of being unfit; Shadrach, a soldier on leave; and he, a soldier sent to escort his CO's wife to the regiment's watering hole.

It was the best he could do. The army was scouring the field for *four* deserters. Only they knew that the fourth had died from both malaria and starvation. He'd died the morning they boarded the train to freedom.

One of the men, a black-bearded man with a fierce set to his mouth, and the unacknowledged leader of the group, fired the question in a heavy, rasping Hindi.

'Which side?'

There was a crash and a bang, and the three soldiers had stood up, upending the table. Most of the noise was Antar's fault but in the dim light of the eatery, the sunlight fell on their dusty faces and their expressions were identical: arrogant and furious.

The townsfolk slowly backed off. Farouk said, his voice hard, 'We're Hindustani. *All of us.*'

Despite their fairly convincing 'histories', no one could deny that it was Farouk's final lie that saved them from being lynched. He shook hands with the others, thanking them for their presence of mind. Shadrach said Farouk owed them, and Antar gave a ghost of the devil's grin.

It wasn't much of a town but it certainly was cut off from the outside world. A ravaged, broken and dirty town, where the houses stood on the edges of the streets, the walls crumbling, their paint chipped by countless bullets, the roofs burnt and blackened by fire.

There was just one two-storeyed motel. Tourism was non-existent because of the war, and they were incredibly fortunate to find a place to stay.

Inside, they could at last speak freely—not in their slightly accented Hindi but in Arabic, *their* language.

Of the four rooms on the top floor, they were generously given the largest. Shadrach hated it at first sight—empty save the mattress that would have only two, and a small cooking stove in the corner. There was a tall pillar in the middle of the floor, but not much else, and the window was almost painted shut.

The view was dreary, of the back garden. It was night at last, the stars almost indiscernible on a spread of black. They'd already eaten in the early evening, and there was nothing left but to sleep.

This was how they were to start their lives as ordinary men with morals and values?

Antar woke up to a dull ache thudding unbearably somewhere within his mangled leg. It had hurt all night, and now it wouldn't let him sleep. He rolled off the floor, grabbing at the wall to help himself up since he was too proud to use his crutches.

Rays of hesitant sunlight were pouring through the window, bringing into focus every drifting particle of dust. In the silent room, it was a hypnotizing sight.

Stepping outdoors was like feeling the breeze in the height of summer: cool and unexpected. It was bright, empty, and as clean as possible but it was so far removed from the motel, its rickety stairs and dark corners and bleak rooms, that *he* felt alive. It was an indescribable sensation, for Shadrach's inexplicable dislike for their accommodations had been contagious.

He suddenly stiffened as he saw someone approach.

Black-bearded. Hard-jawed. Fierce-mouthed. A bear. A pistol-butt visible above the belt of his trousers.

Antar recognized him at once from the day before. Feeling reckless, he raised a hand and waved . To his alarm, the big man came straight at him. With his disabled leg, Antar was in no position to make a run for it. Standing erect, he gripped a peg on the wall behind him for support.

The Bear strode forward until he was right in front of Antar, towering over him. He glowered, and his lips twisted in a snarl that made Antar flinch even though he held his ground. 'What do you want, you bullying toerag?'

The Bear made an inarticulate sound.

Feeling bolder than he should, Antar carried on, 'Yeah—that's right—what right have you got, cornering people in the street, you tea-cultivating bully?'

The Bear said nothing. Did nothing.

But the next thing Antar felt was the pain erupting inside him, piercing his back. The Bear had shoved him hard, flattening him against the peg. 'Watch your mouth!' he growled. 'You're just a gun-toting stranger—watch your dirty, slithering tongue or I'll *slice it off*!'

'*Touchy* . . .' groaned Antar, knees buckling beneath him, unable to stand straight.

Smack.

A fist connected with his jaw. Antar's head flung back and hit the wall. The pain broke out, dizzying. He knew his head was thumping, throbbing but he wasn't bleeding . . .

'*Oye*, Bear,' he mumbled, 'there's blood all over you . . .'

The man stiffened tightly, freezing up as if paralysed. 'My son,' he whispered (Antar *almost* didn't hear him), 'was found buried alive in the mine at dawn.'

Antar swore softly under his breath. Gritting his teeth, he struggled to stand up. The Bear had given up all signs of resuming violence. When Antar turned to glance at him, he was clutching a corner of the wall, blindly staring up the lane.

'One of my friends is a doctor,' said Antar suddenly, not sure why he was volunteering this information. The Bear didn't react. 'He can help you—help your son.'

The Bear slowly raised his head. '*Would* he—?' Hope flickered in him for the life of a son he'd have killed himself to save.

The Bear's wife was a flighty, nervous sparrow. Her face was drawn, pale and bent over the tray she carried, and she said nothing, not a word. Shadrach shrugged, and readily sipped the lemonade she offered them. It was mouth-melting sweet, the sour tang of lemons lost inside it.

The Bear's house was small, the drawing room dark, the sunlight shiftily sneaking between the slats of the drawn blinds. Shadrach and a swollen-faced Antar sat in the chairs with hand-embroidered cushions. The Bear sat opposite them in the wicker armchair, looking blank yet authoritarian. His name was Barua.

Watching the hands folded in his lap, Shadrach wanted to prescribe a hot-water bath for them to prevent callouses. Those hands were cut, bleeding and, some of their bones broken. He wasn't surprised. Barua had tried to rescue his son from beneath a mountain of rubble before help arrived. He'd taken a look at the boy. Lungs choked with dust. Ribs cracked. Superficial head injury. A lot of damage, but the boy would most certainly live. His mother had burst out sobbing when he'd first pronounced his diagnosis, the words loud in the grim silence. It had been difficult to talk inside Barua's house, but Antar wouldn't relent as they made their slow procession to the motel. He'd glimpsed Shadrach's face.

'Would you have rather let that boy die?' he questioned quietly, as soon as they were outdoors.

'Would you have let me?' retorted Shadrach. 'You know I haven't served medical duty in four years—*four years*! That's a lifetime ago, Antar—what if I'd messed up? Do you know what it feels like? To stand in a dark room, with a battered, crumpled 16-year-old in front of you and instruments that feel alien in your hands? Every eye watching you, *believing* in you, and you can't—'

'Rubbish,' snorted Antar, feeling a pang of guilt, nonetheless. 'The Bear would've liked a good excuse to rip your limbs apart.'

It was halfway into the morning by then. People on the streets stopped and stared at the two soldiers.

'I'm *finished*,' Shadrach whispered, angry and frustrated, '*finished* with pretending to be an angel of life.'

'And just what exactly did you do today?' interrupted Antar coldly. 'We're not going back to the battlefield—*ever.* We'd be killed before we got a chance to open our mouths. We have to find a different way of life. We're not mercenaries anymore. And look at you—you're *lamenting* the very fact that you do have something else to do with your self.'

Shadrach snuck a glance at Antar, flinching at the sight of the other's flushed face. 'I'm not—'

But Antar cut him off and went on, ruthless, 'I don't think you realize how many of us would kill to be in your shoes. I know Farouk and I would. I think we'd have left you for the firing squad if we knew you really *were* a coward. I don't have a *leg*—not really. But I don't want to curl up in a ditch and die like a wounded dog. No, I think I'll leave that to you, after all.'

Shadrach froze in his tracks. The blood drained away from his face.

Antar didn't spare him a second glance. He kept on walking, hobbling, stumbling, never stopping, never falling.

The air in their motel room was heavy and clogged with silence. Farouk sat perched on the window sill, his mouth a dour slash, his face cruel.

Having hoped for a semblance of fellow-feeling from him, Shadrach felt he was being judged, being punished, for a good deed now being considered a crime. Who were *they* to judge him? They were all deserters, running from the violence that had become the creed and truth of the world. They were idealists, searching for salvation, but God does forgive sinners like He forgives their sins.

They were *mercenaries*. They were paid in the currency of greed. Paid to destroy. God does not smile upon filth besmirching the earth.

Yet the two of them persisted. Let them, thought Shadrach savagely, *but I know my place. I know that boy could have died as easily as he lived*. Who were the boy's parents to consider him a hero? Who were Antar and Farouk to envy him, call him fortunate? He was damned—and the others, in their envy, were mocking him.

The loud bang of the door jerked him awake.

Antar strode into the room, brushing past Shadrach who stood motionless, arms hanging limply, against the pillar in the middle of the floor. He limped straight to the window. Dimly, Shadrach was aware of Farouk jumping down as well. The heads of the two men were crammed out the window, but Shadrach felt too far removed for curiosity. Curiosity was a sign of life. He felt at that moment devoid of life. He felt very old and very remote.

Loud voices shouting—the sound came to him from so very far away. Farouk was beckoning wildly. Shadrach moved forward, barely aware of his own actions. As he strolled over to the window, Antar grabbed him by the scruff of his neck and pushed his head out.

The sight made a thrill run down Shadrach's spine. A mob had gathered in the street. He was reminded of the day before—again, Barua, 'the Bear', was at the head of the throng. But wait!—the gun was gone from his belt. His heart thumping, Shadrach scanned the faces of the men below.

They seemed to be . . . cheering. Laughing. Grinning up at him, pale and drained and shaking, hanging out the window.

Barua cupped his hands around his mouth and called up: 'We've misjudged you lot, it seems! You're soldiers—but you're not bad.'

Others called up to them. There were lines etched into their faces, lines of hardship, poverty, suffering But there was something alive in their eyes.

None of the three understood Ahomiya. He could hear them, but barely understand what they said.

'Wha—?' but the word never made it out of his mouth. Farouk thumped him so hard on his back it knocked the breath out of him. 'Don't you get it, Shadrach?' he muttered, bringing his mouth close to Shadrach's ear, each word as distinct and glittering as crystal. 'These people accept us because of you. We're people to them, too. Not soldiers. *Persons.*'

'I—I did nothing —'

'You saved a boy's life.'

'So?' he mumbled, still bewildered, giddied by the fierce happiness shining in the faces of these once-hostile townsfolk. 'They have doctors here, too.'

'Not surgeons', said Antar softly, 'not *surgeons.* And that's what they think you are. The pinnacle of medical greatness. The miracle-worker.'

Slowly, Shadrach turned to look at him. There was no expression, no envy, no mockery in that face. He glanced back at Farouk who met his gaze calmly, smiling. They were simply reciting the facts to him.

Only later—seconds later, seconds that melted into eternity —did realization sink in, like treacle laced with poison.

Still standing at the window, Shadrach whispered hollowly, voicing the very words none of them wanted to hear, 'We can't take this any further.'

Antar let out a bark of derisive laughter. 'Take *what*?' he questioned harshly, 'You boot-polishing little idealist.'

'Back off,' commanded Farouk sharply. 'Lay off him, Antar. He's right and you know it, and you know it's not a question of idealism. We can't do this—can't go on deceiving them.'

Buoyed by the support, Shadrach added quickly, 'They have a *right* to know.'

Farouk glanced at him, but said nothing.

'So, what?' said Antar, fighting to keep himself under control, 'We just march down there, show them our rifles and tell them, *Listen up, chaps, we're really Egyptian. We're scum, the blot on the world's embellished moral system*. Is that what you want, Farouk? The only way you'll get us out of this is with more lies. And that's what you do best, isn't it?'

Farouk stiffened. His eyes blazed with a hard, cold rage. 'Sometimes, lies can save your *life*,' he bit out tersely, 'and remember that they also saved *yours*, before you talk to me with *your* embellished moral system.'

Antar sneered. 'Are you being *honest* here, Farouk? Are you really saying what you mean? Because I always find that hard to believe. I've never heard you talk like that. Silver-tongued, we call you, and that's your pride, isn't it?'

'Shut up,' barked a voice suddenly. It was Shadrach.

The two men were staring at him, at the sudden tight edge to his voice. Antar's lip curled, but he said nothing. This time. His words were only his shield. Suddenly, he felt too tired to shield himself anymore.

Down on the street, it felt like they were walking into an arena. There were 50 people, looking at them with blatant curiosity and admiration and dissolving distrust. Antar and Shadrach exchanged glances, moving aside to let Farouk step forward. Barua materialized to grasp his hand tightly in a grateful, pleased shake.

Farouk's skin tingled, his mouth grew dry as rasped out the words, unflinchingly looking Barua in the eye, 'There are things you need to know about us.'

Barua's eyes narrowed at once. The old distrust flooded back. It was Shadrach he had trusted so far. Perhaps Antar and Farouk had never been on his list . . .

Farouk started speaking very fast. 'We aren't the soldiers you thought us to be. We're not even Indian. We're African mercenaries from the battlefront at Kargil. We're—' Something seemed to be lodged in his throat, making it impossible to pronounce that word: *deserters*.

The crowd behind Barua began talking loudly, all at once. Only Barua had heard, only he understood. And he had gone very still, his forehead a dangerous crag leaning over the film slipping over his dark eyes.

'Hired killers,' he said softly.

Farouk swallowed. He glanced over his shoulder at the other two men, standing, waiting for judgement. He saw Antar incline his head in secret assent.

'Not all of us,' he said. 'Only Antar and I. Shadrach's an army surgeon.'

Barua still said nothing. But Shadrach had heard.

'*No*!' he yelled in his native tongue. '*Don't—*!'

He lunged forward, but Antar caught him as he leapt, restraining him with an inhuman strength he'd mustered out of nowhere. '*Don't be stupid, man,*' he snarled. 'This is your one chance to start afresh.'

'*No,*' shouted Shadrach, not flinching from the stares. '*No, no, no*—I don't want it. I'm not leaving you two.'

Antar hit him, his fist connecting hard with Shadrach's belly as one foot ground into Shadrach's. The pain erupted in his skull and Shadrach doubled over, falling on his knees in a painful crouch. Farouk, who'd been watching, coolly turned away to face the dark aura of Barua.

'Antar and I are leaving,' he said. 'We apologize for our intrusion—'

Tears of pain splintering his eyes, Shadrach croaked out in his broken Hindi, 'I'm coming too—' But right beside him, Antar's throat exploded in a cough, and barely anyone heard.

But there would be no more deception. It would be as simple as that.

Shadrach stared down at the ground to avoid looking at anyone. His heart was thudding. Did he really have to leave? He thought of Barua's son, the first person he had healed, and of all the other people he could help some day . . . all the other people in this remote town who needed him to help them . . .

If there were to be no more deceptions, perhaps he had a reason to stay.

The words sounded odd. He glanced up slowly, realizing he'd said those words aloud. Every one was looking only at him.

Their only sign of parting were the footprints in the dust at the old station. No one came to see them off, save Shadrach. He stood on the platform, saying nothing, his hand lifted in farewell, as he watched Farouk help a grudging Antar board. He had nothing to say—nothing left to say— because he'd said it all, and goodbye was meant to be sweet without the 'bitter'.

The two of them had found their pinprick of light in thc tunnel, and Shadrach had found his too. They parted as friends, soon to be strangers—men who had started off as deserters, now to be redeemed. The war was not over. But for these men, peace had come early.

THE HOME YOU LEFT BEHIND

Prithwish Nath
16 YEARS
NATIONAL GEMS HIGHER SECONDARY SCHOOL, CALCUTTA

Max made his way nervously up the rugged side of the hill, his gun ready. He glanced around him every now and then, licking his dry lips, his face expressionless. From time to time he gulped nervously and raised a gloved hand to wipe the sweat off his neck. 'On your guard, lads!' he barked out to his squad. 'Look sharp!' The haggard lot stumbled on, kicking debris out of their way. It's been five years since any of them stepped out into the open. Not since the heavy reverses suffered by the Terrans and Vasudans in the Terran–Vasudan war, after which soldiers from both sides retreated into kilometre-wide underground bunkers and the war was carried on by robots. The humans underground were informed of progress via video broadcasts from the robots. Now, the Terran High Command had issued directives to scout the surface perimeter, and it had fallen on Max and his squad, the 42nd Ravens, to undertake the job.

The group, now edgy, was almost at the top of the hill. Nothing could be seen beyond it. They would have to cross to the other side. Max reached the top and came face to face with a squad of Vasudans and instantly, 30 pairs of guns went up, aimed at each other. Though no one willing to fire first lest he meet the same fate seconds later.

'Surrender, or die!' spat the Vasudan commander in Max's face, the barrel of his handgun against Max's temple. 'Likewise,' smirked Max, pressing his own against his counterpart's forehead.

'Cease and desist! Stop your futile argument!'—a mechanical voice interrupted the standoff. They were the robots—but . . . something was wrong . . . both the Terran and the Vasudan robots had interrupted them instead of fighting.

'Terran Mech Unit! What is the meaning of this?'

'Vasudan Mech Unit, this calls for an explanation!'

The respective commanders barked at their machines.

'All will be explained in time. For now, simply come with us' came the unemotional metallic reply.

'Where?' enquired Max.

'To the home you left behind.'

The cityscape, smouldering, desolate, ruined, the buildings standing like yellowed skulls—that is what the war had turned their earth into. But what was this? Lush, green, flowing meadows, rivers with crystal clear water running through them. In the distance, dense green forests.

'H . . . how could this happen?' stammered Max.

'We have been rebuilding earth' answered the mechanical voice. 'Realizing the futility of war, the Terran and Vasudan robots made peace and combined their technology to create Nanobots to undo the destruction you and your kind have wrecked upon this rich planet.'

'B . . . but what about the video broadcasts you've been sending us? About the progress of the war?'

'Fake messages, designed to keep humans in their bunkers, to prevent further wars,' came the answer.

'No, no, no! This is not possible!' cried out the Vasudan Commander.

'Why not?' said a slightly shaken Max. 'We created them, we've been striving to make them better, more . . . human. Well, they're human now. More, much more than any of us . . .' His face was wet with tears. 'Much more. For they have realized the futility of war—the pain, the destruction it causes. "To the home you left behind." Our home, our planet, our source of life and we squandered it away over our petty differences. Our hatred for each other. No doubt, they're undoubtedly more human than us!'

'All hope is not yet lost,' the robot said. 'This rebuilding can continue on a much larger scale once we have the support of your scientists and their knowledge. Call your superiors. Let them know what has transpired. There is still hope for mankind.'

'Yes, yes! We will cooperate! Mankind will rise once again to it's previous glory. Like a child learning from a mistake, like a phoenix from the ashes, it will be reborn! If robots can understand the importance of peace, can not the humans? Are we so intent on destroying each other that we can no longer make room in our hearts for love?'

'. . . and as these events transpired, the headquarters of both forces received such emotionally overcome messages, reporting an impossible scenario but supporting it with very real video evidence. What reactions it may have brought forth I don't know, but it prompted the leaders to end the war once and for all, and contribute to making a better world for all of us—'

Thus concluded Max, now at the ripe old age of 73, narrating the story of earth's rebirth to his grandchildren.

'That was the best story we've every heard, Grandpa! Tell us another!'

'All right, children, that's enough, give Grandpa some peace and quiet now!' said their mother, smiling, and took them into the house.

Sitting outside, in the bright, sunny, beautiful morning, smiling to himself, Max thought, 'Life always finds a way. Yes, life will always find a way . . .'.

THE OLD LADY

Saamidheni Das
15 YEARS
BIRLA HIGH SCHOOL (GIRLS' SECTION), CALCUTTA

The faint rays of daylight has just cleared the dark sky. Colonel Abhay Batra sat on the wooden bench at the side of the park and stared at the grass. It was around 4.30 a.m. Colonel Batra was a retired army man. He has been sitting on this bench, at this time, every day for the past four years.

Today, he remembered, was a very special day in his life—'10th of May,' he muttered to himself.

Abhay Batra, out of immense love and respect for his motherland, had joined the Indian Army. He was an admirable human being. He had wanted peace—in his country and in the world at large. And he was ready to sacrifice his life for his country and for peace.

The tall and slightly bent figure of Colonel Batra touched his hair, now greying, and tried to recall an image of his younger self. A tall and fair man, his small eyes full of courage and confidence, he always had a little smile at the corner of his lips. Although an old man now, he still had courage of thought and action.

'Twenty-five years,' said Colonel Batra to himself. 'Will I never meet her again? My mother?' A tear rolled down his cheek. Now, slowly, he remembered that face, that smile, those eyes and the love of a mother. As he went back 25 years, he felt a surge of happiness well up in his heart.

Abhay Batra had been only 29 then. A young and brave soldier in the Indian Army. There were no troubles near the borders. No one thought such a thing could happen. But, all of a sudden, the army was put on alert: dangerous terrorists had entered the country. Like all other soldiers, Abhay was also informed and he bravely volunteered to join the anti-terrorist squad.

It was a dangerous mission. The soldiers fought the terrorists tooth and nail. Bombs exploded, bullets whizzed through the air. Though some terrorists were killed, many soldiers also died.

Then, that day. 10 May. It was reported that the few surviving terrorists had decided to plant bombs in important public places. 'We will stop them,' promised the soldiers. The terrorist hideout was discovered and both groups of men fired at each other for three hours. Abhay was part of that mission too. Suddenly, he heard a gunshot and the next moment a terrible pain seared through him, near his right shoulder and his chest. Another gunshot, and this time the pain in his left leg. Then nothing.

When Abhay opened his eyes, he was wracked with pain. 'Oh God . . .' he gasped. At least he had not gone blind. He closed his eyes again. The faint sounds of a woman's voice came to his ears. A thought struck him. 'Where am I? Home? No . . . what is . . .' he tried to think. He opened his eyes once more and cried out faintly, 'Father.'

Abhay had never seen his mother. His father had been the only person, surrounding him entirely. Now he saw a pair of eyes looking at him—eyes with so much love and care in them. He realized he was somewhere else, and there was a woman looking at him. She was about 50 and Abhay felt he had known her for a very long time. 'Where am I? Who are you? How did you . . . ?' Abhay asked her.

Before Abhay finished, she said, 'Son, you are in my house. Don't worry. You were hit by two bullets but the doctors have operated and taken them out. You will be fine in a few more days. Think of this as your home and of me as your mother.' Tears rolled down her cheeks as she spoke. Abhay asked no more questions. The woman took care of him and he began to understand a mother's love. 'Who am I to her? Why is she looking after me? She gave me a second birth by saving my life. She is my mother,' Abhay said to himself. And so a week passed.

The bond between Abhay and the lady grew strong. Then, one day, an elderly man came to him and said he was absolutely fine and that he could go back home. He was the lady's husband. 'I do not know how to thank you. I am very grateful to you, Mother. I will leave tomorrow,' Abhay said to the lady who had looked after him.

Tears welled up in her eyes. 'What is it, Mother?' asked Abhay. 'You may go, son, but how will you understand a mother's worry for her child? Those terrorists you were fighting are also dead. There is peace now. But so many sons sacrificed their lives and made their parents cry. Can all this fighting never stop? Can't there be peace, love and respect in the world?' Abhay had no answer. The lady spoke again, 'You are also my son. My second son. My elder son gave up his life, but not as a soldier, as a terrorist, five years ago.'

'A terrorist?' asked Abhay he was shocked.

'Yes. He thought he could bring peace that way. But he was wrong. True peace can come only through love, respect and humanity. Religion, class, caste, society—all these are made by humans and now we tend to respect these more than we do each other as human beings. Why don't we forget all this and hold each other's hand as friends? Then no mother will have to cry for her child.'

They did not talk any more. Abhay returned home full of love and respect for his 'mother'.

Many years passed. It had been on 10 May that he had met someone through whom he could recognize a mother, through whom he got the love of a mother and for whom he promised to bring peace in the world. He knew he could not do it alone, but he tried to do all that he could so that others could be inspired. Slowly, he had become Colonel Abhay Batra. Slowly, he had become old.

'I don't know where my mother is today, but I will do all to bring about the peace she wanted. I cannot do it in my lifetime, but someone after me perhaps can bring true peace and make my mother's dream come true.' Colonel Batra stood up. It was almost 6.00 a.m. The birds had come out. The day was shining. He started walking slowly, his heart happy and his eyes started shining with a bright hope.

THE STARS PLAY FOOTBALL

Aparna Gupta
17 YEARS
CAMBRIDGE SCHOOL, SRINIVASPURI, NEW DELHI

It was a still summer night. As the train moved past the grasslands, hills and villages, people dozed in their compartments. But one traveller was awake. Kathy, a plump woman of about 30, was sitting beside the window, reading a book by the dim light of the lamp. Even if she had wanted to sleep, she would not have been able to because of the commotion the children opposite her were making. Kathy glanced at them. A boy of about four and a girl, about six, with their mother.

'Don't look out of the window,' the mother shouted at the boy.

'Mamma, where were the stars and the moon when we were dressing up in the morning? Where do they go away during the day?' the boy asked.

'Stupid! They're always there. They just play hide and seek with us. If you catch them, then you can hide and they will have to seek you,' his sister told him with an air of infinite knowledge.

'One day I'll catch the moon,' the boy said with great determination. And then began a long discussion about where they would hide so that the moon couldn't catch them.

But Kathy heard them no more. Their chatter had taken her back . . . into the past . . .

A little girl, running down the street. Huffing and puffing, she reaches the town park and approaches a little boy sitting on the swing.

'Imran! The stars are lost! Somebody has stolen them! I saw them at night, but now they're gone!'

'Don't be silly, Kathy. The stars aren't lost. Do you expect them to hang from the sky all day? They have to go to school, eat lunch, play football and then come back at night,' the boy says with that 'I-know-it-all' air.

'Oh!' Kathy mulls the thought. 'But they mustn't play football. I don't like football.'

'Stupid! Stars aren't girls. They're boys and they like to play football.'

'If Imran says the stars are boys, they must be,' thinks Kathy loyally. 'Imran knows everything. He can add two-digit numbers and spell words like "choir" and "classic."' Kathy does not know what they mean, but they sound difficult. And Imran is always right.

Yes, for little Kathy, Imran was always right. He was the most intelligent person she knew—after her father, of course 'Because Daddy knows even more than Imran. He can even cover my books.'

Four-year-old Kathy and seven-year-old Imran were good friends. They had been neighbours since Kathy was a year old and her father had brought her to this town after her mother died. It was Imran who had told her that they were neighbours.

'You know, Kathy,' he said one day, 'I'm your neighbour.'

'What's that?

'I don't know. My mother said I was your neighbour. Maybe best friends are called neighbours,' five-year-old Imran replied solemnly.

'Then I'm your neighbour too!' exclaimed Kathy happily.

Imran was Kathy's idol, friend, brother—everything. And for Imran, Kathy was the little sister he never had. They were inseparable. Years passed by and Kathy turned eight.

One day, civil war broke out. People started killing each other in the name of God and religion. Curfew was imposed in town.

'But I want to go outside. I haven't played with Imran for two days now. I want to show him my new drawing,' Kathy cried.

'My dear, we can't go out now. There's a war on,' her father tried to explain.

'What's a war, Daddy?'

'When people fight with each other.'

'But I fight with Imran all the time . . .'

'No dear, this is when grown-ups fight with guns and bombs and we cannot go out of our houses.'

'I hate wars. Why do we have wars?' Kathy cried.

Kathy shed silent tears before falling off to sleep. It had been difficult for her father to explain. But he had far more important things to worry about. They would soon have to leave the country—it was becoming difficult for foreigners to stay in this land. But how could he tell his little girl that she couldn't meet her best friend anymore?

Imran's parents helped them escape. It was tough separating the two children from each other.

'Why can't Kathy live with us?'

'When will I meet Imran again?'

The day of parting arrived. The children had no words to speak and tears flowed down their cheeks. Kathy gave all her precious drawings to her friend and he gave her his favourite marbles. Then they waved goodbye to each other until they could see each other no more . . .

Years have passed but the memories are still fresh in her mind. It seems only yesterday that a little girl worried about the stars being lost. Even now she could not understood fundamentalism nor why people fought wars nor why they could not live in peace and harmony . . .

Kathy was brought back to the present as the train stopped at her station. As she stood up to leave, she said to the little boy, 'You know, my dear, the stars play football in the daytime.'

Clutching her bag and her memories of Imran to her chest, Kathy stepped onto the platform.

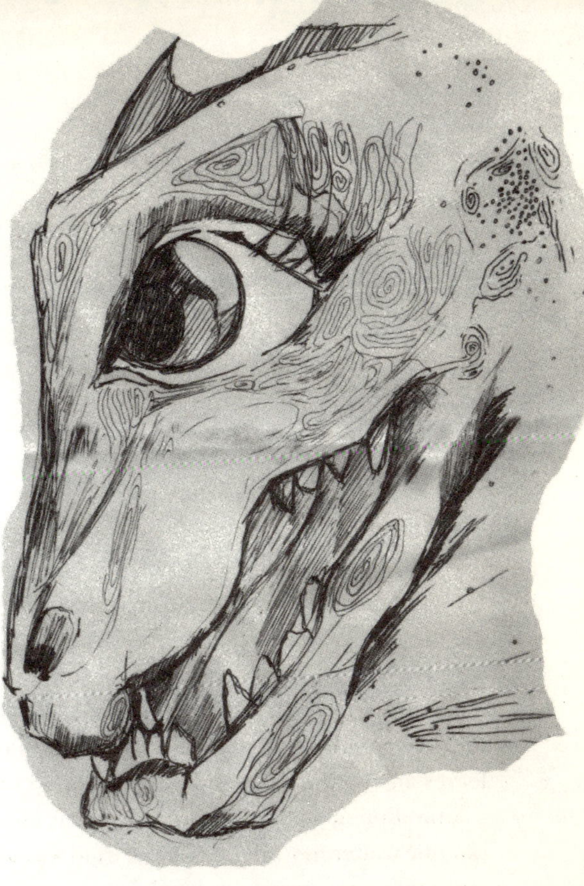

THE (VERY) FIRST WORLD WAR

Anasua Chatterjee
18 YEARS
MAHEDEVI BIRLS GIRLS HIGHER SECONDARY SCHOOL, CALCUTTA

He had little feet. Not *that* little of course, but, well, smaller than the others. So he was called Littlefoot. Kindly, you understand because he was Dextra's son and Dextra was the herd mother, but also because he was a happy and lovable fellow to begin with. He played games well, had the best nose for elderberry leaves among the herd, and was good at everything expected of a little dinosaur 10 years old. But this is about what Littlefoot saw one winter morning, when the wind was blowing swiftly, flattening his ears against his head.

He'd gone to a particularly low bunch of elderberry leaves which didn't give him a crick in the neck (his neck wasn't long yet, only about a hundred twigs or so), and was happily chomping away when there was this noise. It wasn't a very strange noise, just a far off rumble, but his mother wasn't the herd mother for nothing and had taught him that all noises were potential sources of danger. They did usually turn out to be little Samba trying to scare him or something but . . . Unwillingly, he left a half-munched leaf and walked to the edge of the glade. And saw a very strange sight.

It had all started last winter. Food hadn't been plentiful, and a bunch of Heavytop troublemakers had started talking about how the Longtops were responsible for being so huge, eating too much and clearing all the vegetation. Littlefoot was a Longtop and he knew it was all bosh, of course. The Heavytops ate just as much. They'd just wanted an excuse to start something. Actually, their power-hungry leader, Gor, *was* looking to start something and the others had just played along. And then Dextra'd said a few cutting things about the Heavytops' appetite, and the battle lines were drawn, even though they'd lived happily since before anyone could remember. Even Littlefoot's friend Fuzzytop's family had turned against them. And Fuzzy couldn't remember why, because Littlefoot had often gone over to their home for dinner and his mother had plied him with food, saying he didn't eat enough. It was all very queer.

Soon, Fuzzy, the best Rockshoot player in the valley, wasn't allowed to play with them anymore. And the Heavytops had gone away in rancour, and Eldervalley was left to the Longtops. Through the valley and all through dinosaurland, as far as the sea, there had been rumblings of menace and stray fights, even rumours of interbreed wars. And Dextra started going around with a worried look. And though Littlefoot missed Fuzzy, the food had all grown back in spring as everyone should have known it would. Plus he was a resilient little dinosaur and he got over the loss with the coming of the long, meandering, indolent days of summer. Until today. Because, on that crisp winter day, he saw the Eldervalley Rockshooting champion Fuzzy Heavytop running towards him. Fuzzy had blood all over his wide, good-natured face. It ran off in tiny rivulets, and fell on the trampled grass as he ran towards Littlefoot, the ground shaking beneath his panicked feet. He was running so fast that he banged into Littlefoot and got blood all over him as well. 'Fuzz, you're not supposed to be here! We'll both get into trouble . . . and how in blazes did you get like this?' Fuzzy took a few deep breaths. 'Gor hit me with his tail. I ran away, and then I thought I'd . . . warn you. Littlefoot, they're going to kill you all.'

The world seemed to stop. The silence echoed in Littlefoot's ears. His first thought was that his mother had been right when she made everyone take precautions and arrange hiding places. And his second thought, as he heard the crashing noises in the undergrowth, was that they wouldn't have time to get there. He grabbed Fuzzy, his friend and now inexplicably his enemy, and they hid behind a tree as the first of the Heavytops ran by. It was Fuzzy's uncle, Joker, his face twisted with an insane rage.

Uncle Joker, who, true to his name, had always laughed with them and coached them in the intricacies of Rockshoot.

There was little to be gained by warning anyone, but Littlefoot and Fuzzy ran through the secret path known only to the young, and reached Dextra in the main plain. But Dextra already had her nose to the wind. She lowered her immense neck and looked at Littlefoot long and hard, as if to memorize his dear face and the look in her eyes held all the sadness in the world and froze him to his bones. Then she said just one word, 'Go'. And he knew it meant nothing would ever be the same again. It was the only thing she had ever made him promise her. That if she said 'go', he would gather the children and go to the secret cave in the hillside. And not emerge until . . . well, he would know when. She hadn't said any more, just hugged him fiercely until he groaned 'Ma!' and shrugged her off, a faint sense of fear overlaying his annoyance.

Chaos burst open on the plain. Littlefoot and Fuzzy gathered the children while his mother talked to the adults in the tone which usually made him proud of her. Now it just scared him, and he hurried the younger ones to the hills and left them in the cave with Fuzzy. He came out to the cliff edge, meaning to ask his mother a few questions, uneasily remembering Uncle Joker's bloodthirsty face, and inadvertently saw the first Heavytop crashing through the shade trees. It was Gor, his face lit up with a maniacal glee as he lashed out with his spiked tail at the first Longtop he could see. A deep red gash opened in the dinosaur's chest, and the first drops of blood stained the green floor of the valley. Littlefoot had seen what his mother would have spared him the sight of. Somehow, he knew that this was the end of the world as he knew it and trod dazedly back to the cave. He felt nothing but regret that it had happened this way. And a faint sense of surprise—even while the carnage went on below, he felt no anger for Fuzzy whose face mirrored his own. Even now, he could find no difference between the two of them except that Fuzzy could play Rockshoot better, but only because his feet were larger. He knew that when the pain hit he would scream. But now he was numb. Dead inside.

It was two days and two nights before they could emerge. And Dextra had been right. He had known when—when the sounds died. They were hidden downwind, but they had heard a few screams. The young ones had paled and retreated further into the cave, crying now and then but stopping when the elders took no notice. Tears were too easy for grief such as this.

Littlefoot herded everyone outside, through another path, because there was really no point in going back. The swarming pterodactyls told him that, though he tried not to see them and tried not to think.

It was three days before they came within stone's throw of the neighbouring herd of Longtops.

The silence in this valley told Littlefoot all he wanted to know. He and Fuzzy stopped the others and walked onto the plain. They stopped when they saw the first one. Lying on the ground, twisted, his eyes glazed over. A Heavytop, but to them it didn't matter. He was just confirmation of what they would find in their homes. They turned away. There was no need to go any further. Indeed, Littlefoot did not know where they would go. He knew that what had happened marked the end of their kind. He wondered what explanation would later be found to account for such a downfall.

And as he stood there on the plain stained red, he wondered desperately, as other living beings would, later in time, whether anybody would ever realize what this pain was like before they set out to kill, to maim. And remembering Uncle Joker's wild face as he charged, he didn't think they would. He didn't think they would ever learn.

He was right.

TO THE ROOTS OF PEACE

Dipti Shah
18 YEARS
BIRLA HIGH SCHOOL (GIRLS' SECTION), CALCUTTA

A young man, Ian, married a woman whose brother, Adam, was blind. Ian was eager to get to know his new brother-in-law, so he invited him to go hunting.

Adam replied, 'I cannot see, remember? But if you help me, I will enjoy our time together.'

Ian led Adam into the forest. At first, they followed a path that the blind man knew and the journey was easy for him. After a while, though, the brush got thicker, the trees grew closer together and there were many places for the animals to hide.

Adam now held on to Ian's arm. He told him many things about the sounds they heard around them. Because he had no sight, he had a great ability to interpret the noises made by animals in the bush.

'There are some creatures there . . . Hyenas I guess. I can hear them, over there.' Pointing at the noise he took a few steps, then pointed elsewhere and said, 'There! That bird is preparing to fly. Listen to the sound of its wings unfolding.' 'These sounds are meaningless to me,' Ian confessed. 'You can understand the bush in a way that is beyond me!'

They walked on for several hours until they came to the water. Ian said this was a good place to set their traps. 'The birds will come for water here,' he said.

Ian put his trap a short distance away, taking care to disguise it well. He did not bother to hide Adam's trap—it was hot and he was eager to get home to his new wife. When Ian urged Adam to follow, the blind man came willingly, believing Ian had hidden his trap well. They went home. The next day, they returned to their traps. Adam was excited at the thought of having caught something and Ian had to tell him to keep quiet or he would scare the animals away. Even before they reached the traps, Adam could tell they had been lucky: 'I can hear birds! There are birds in the traps!' His voice was so full of excitement! When he reached his trap, Ian saw he had caught a small grey bird. He took it out of the trap and put it in a pouch that he had brought with him. Then they walked towards Adam's.

Ian said, 'You've caught one too' and all at once he was filled with envy. Adam's bird was marvellously coloured, as if it had flown through a rainbow and been stained by the hues. The feathers from a bird like that would make a fine present for his new wife. Ian quickly switched the birds, then said. 'Here's yours.'

Adam felt the bird for a moment, his fingers passing over the wings and the breast. Then, silently, he put the bird into his pouch. The two began the trip home. They talked for many hours, of many things, then stopped for a rest under a tree. Ian asked Adam, 'You are so wise. You know so many things even though you see nothing at all. There is something that has always troubled me—why do people fight with one another?'

Adam took his time, then turned to Ian as if he could see and said, 'Men fight because they do to each other what you have just done to me.'

Ashamed, Ian rose to his feet, fetched his pouch, took out the brightly coloured bird, and gave it back to Adam.

Adam felt the bird, then smiled and said, 'Do you have any other questions for me?'

This time Ian asked, shamefully, 'Yes. How do men become friends again?'

Adam smiled. 'They do what you have just done to me.'

THE WHITE CITY

Damini Agarwal
14 YEARS
NATIONAL GEMS HIGHER SECONDARY SCHOOL, CALCUTTA

We've all heard of the Pink City and the Blue City, haven't we? It's 2100 and we now have a White City. What's so special about it? We know all the buildings are pink in the Pink City. So in the White City are they all white? No. The White City is the most peaceful city in the world and is located on an equally peaceful location—the Moon.

All the houses are shaped in the form of peace symbols—doves, olive twigs and crosses. The sky is light blue with wisps of white clouds and a permanent silver lining. The trees are laden with fruits and birds twitter melodiously. People speak in soft whispers and not a single rude word escapes their lips. Machines work soundlessly, cars don't blow their horns and faithfully obey radar signals.

There are no punishments for wrongdoers because there are none. If someone happens to commit a crime, the people wait for the goodness of the city to take its toll on the wrongdoer.

There are a series of paths connecting the earth to the White City—one from each continent. These paths are made of gold and silver and have huge trees growing along their sides. The golden path leads to the destructive Black City and the silver to the calm White City.

Once, accidentally, Osama Bin Laden wandered into the White City. He mistook the silver path as the one leading to the Black City and landed up with his goons. He was astounded to see what lay around him. He had been told that the Black City was a mirror of hell but this place looked more like heaven. 'Must be some idiotic rumour,' he grumbled. Then, one by one he called his goons and instructed them, 'Search this whole place. Don't leave a single stone unturned. Come and tell me what you see.' 'Now,' he thought, 'I'll go in search of some guns.' He had not brought any with him since the Black City was rumoured to be the best place for them.

Bin Laden set off and went to every shop in the city but all he got was peaceful smiles and confused looks. Angrily, he thumped his fist on the shop counters, 'WHERE ARE ALL THE GUNS I WAS PROMISED AND WHY ARE YOU ALL STAR-

ING AT ME?' The shopkeeper looked him in the eye and said calmly, 'There are none here.' Bin Laden wanted to shout some more but the quiet and firm answer of the shopkeeper stopped him and he stomped out of the shop. Soon his henchmen returned and confirmed that there were indeed no guns available. Worse—All exits to this city are closed,' one of them said, 'the roads are being repaired and they don't want people like us wandering in all the time.' Frustrated, dejected and horrified at the thought of no guns, Bin Laden began to weep.

The citizens grew worried and whispered to one another.

'Is he ill?'

'He needs flowers, you know, they're a marvelous cure.'

'Is he in love?' asked one man who came forward and gently patted him on the back, 'Don't worry, my dear, you'll meet your girl soon enough. The exits aren't closed forever.' They showered him with bouquets and cards to cheer him up but he looked at them blankly. By the time he came into his senses and decided to explain, the crowd had dispersed. Only his men were left, sniggering. Bin Laden walked into a hotel, shut himself up and, to his dismay, found that the room had been lined with flowers and cards. He flopped onto his bed and looked gloomily around him. Then finally fell asleep.

The next day he was more careful of his actions in public and behaved in a comparatively more serene manner. His goons aped their master. People came to cheer him up again and he said 'Thank you' very graciously and with a big smile.

Many days passed. The city slowly took its toll on him. Once he saw a line of ants in his path. He walked gingerly around them it, careful not to step on any, and instructed his men, 'Make sure you don't hurt these tiny creatures.' They looked at each other, shrugged their shoulders, then did as they were told. Another day he refused to kill a mosquito and told his men, in all seriousness, 'We don't have the right to destroy anything we can't create ourselves.' They nodded in complete agreement. Though extremely comic events, the citizens of the White City understood their importance and smiled to themselves.

Thus Bin Laden became a changed man.

But the story does not end here. It is rumoured that both Bin Laden and George Bush have been spotted, walking hand in hand, into the sunset, towards the Sea of Tranquility.

PARTICIPATING SCHOOLS

Akshar, Calcutta

Birla Girls High School, Calcutta

Cambridge School, Ghaziabad

Cambridge School, Indirapuram, New Delhi

Cambridge School, Srinivaspuri, New Delhi

Cambridge School, Noida

Cambridge School, Shrinivaspuri, New Delhi

Fr Agnel Multipurpose School, Navi Mumbai

G.D. Birla Centre for Education, Calcutta

Hiranadani Foundation, Navi Mumbai

Karachi High School, Karachi

Lady Andal Venkatasubba Rao School, Chennai

Loreto Day School, Bowbazar, Calcutta

Loreto House, Calcutta

Mahadevi Birla Girls' Higher Secondary School, Calcutta

National Gems Higher Secondary School, Calcutta

Nepali Girls' Higher Secondary School, Darjeeling

Raja Ram Mohan Roy Academy, Dehradun

Salamat Girls ICAS, Lahore

South Point High School, Calcutta

Spastics Society of India, National Resource Centre, Mumbai

Springdales School, New Delhi

Smt. Sulochna Singhania School, Thane

St Teresa's School, Darjeeling

St Xavier's Collegiate School, Calcutta

The British School, New Delhi

The Calcutta Girls High School, Calcutta

The Cambridge School, Calcutta

JUDGES

ANJUM KATYAL is a writer and editor based in Calcutta. She has also translated several plays.

DARCY COURTEAU has a Master of Fine Arts in Fiction from Arizona State University. She conducted the Creative Writing Workshop at the Seagull Arts and Media Resource Centre, Calcutta, on 21 and 22 July 2007 and on 27 and 28 July 2007.

LIZ WIMBERLY has a Master of Fine Arts in Fiction from Arizona State University. She conducted the Creative Writing Workshop at the Seagull Arts and Media Resource Centre, Calcutta, on 21 and 22 July 2007 and on 27 and 28 July 2007.

PeaceWorks

AN INITIATIVE OF THE SEAGULL FOUNDATION FOR THE ARTS

The upsurge of sectarian violence in the country has brought home how imperative it is for all democratic-minded citizens of India to work towards reaffirming and strengthening the fundamental values of our Constitution, which gurantees basic human rights to every citizen, regardless of caste or creed. It is essential to help children and young people, our future citizens, build an attitude of respect and dignity for all faiths and backgrounds.

We at Seagull are concerned about how the space for creative arts and creative expression has been squeezed out of the daily lives of our children, and turned into extra-curricular ephemera delegated to whatever little free time the children might have between tuitions and tests. We feel that the lack of opportunity for creative expression, imaginative thinking, aesthetic appreciation, may be distorting their development as well-rounded individuals or stunting their leadership abilities.

The PeaceWorks Initiative by the Seagull Foundation for the Arts is conceived as a programme that grounds itself in arts and culture but works in the area of civil society and education. This programme envisages a range of projects with the overall aim of building peace, of helping strengthen values of mutual coexistence and respect for all communities.

We invite your cooperation and involvement to help us plan, organize and generate activities as the year progresses.

THE SEAGULL FOUNDATION FOR THE ARTS
36C. S. P. MUKHERJEE ROAD
CALCUTTA 700 025
E-MAIL: peaceworks@seagullindia.com
PHONE: 2455 6942 / 43
www.seagullindia.com